VIRAGO
MODERN CLASSICS
95

Rosamond Lehmann

Rosamond Lehmann (1901–1990) was born in Buckinghamshire. She was educated privately and was a scholar at Girton College, Cambridge. She wrote her first novel in her twenties, the best-selling *Dusty Answer*, and married Wogan Philipps, the artist, in 1928. Her reputation was firmly established with the publication of *A Note in Music* in 1930, and the subsequent *Invitation to the Waltz* and its sequel, *The Weather in the Streets*. During the war she contributed short stories to the notable book-periodical *New Writing* which was edited by her brother, John Lehmann. Rosamond Lehmann remains one of the most distinguished novelists of this century, and was created a CBE in 1982.

Titles by Rosamond Lehmann

Dusty Answer
A Note in Music
Invitation to the Waltz
The Weather in the Streets
No More Music
The Ballad and the Source
The Gypsy's Baby
The Echoing Grove
The Swan in the Evening
A Sea-Grape Tree

A SEA-GRAPE TREE

A SEA-GRAPE TREE

Rosamond Lehmann

*With an Introduction
by Janet Watts*

*With a postscript by
the Author*

For Hugo and Mollie
with love

A *Virago* Book

Published by Virago Press Limited 1982

Reprinted 1985, 1989, 1993, 1998

First published in Great Britain by William Collins Ltd 1976

A CIP catalogue record for this book is available
from the British Library

ISBN 0 86068 335 4

Printed and bound in Great Britain by
Clays Ltd, St Ives plc

Virago
A Division of
Little, Brown and Company (UK)
Brettenham House
Lancaster Place
London WC2E 7EN

INTRODUCTION

Considerable time and a great change separate Rosamond Lehmann's seventh novel from her sixth. *The Echoing Grove* was published in 1953 to wide acclaim, its popularity and critical success confirming and enhancing Miss Lehmann's already-established position among the leading writers of her time. Yet for the next two decades this most loved and respected novelist wrote no word of fiction.

The sudden death of Rosamond Lehmann's daughter Sally in 1958 was not only the most appalling catastrophe of her mother's life. It was to bring about another death: for it ended the life that Rosamond Lehmann had lived until that event – although in that end there was also a new beginning. Before Sally's death, Rosamond Lehmann had shared (although with misgivings) the scepticism and atheism of her generation. After it, she came (to some extent, against her will) slowly to believe, and later to investigate, the existence of other worlds of reality and other levels of experience beyond those of our mortal and material life on earth.

She does not call her exploration 'spiritualism'. She does not like the word, with its associations of trickery, side-shows and silliness. But in these years, Rosamond Lehmann has undergone spiritual experiences that have changed every aspect of her life and outlook. She says simply: 'I now know, with my own certainty, that we do survive death.' It is a realisation that she has won at a considerable cost. She has given her time and energy, her intellect and her heart to this quest; and in its course she has sacrificed both her ambition and her pride.

In *A Sea-Grape Tree* Rosamond Lehmann emerges from her years of literary silence as both a different woman and a different writer. As she says: 'My new outlook and my new knowledge make it, in a way, even more difficult for me to write novels. I now find my earlier novels romantic and melancholy and essentially pessimistic – all of which has become rather foreign to me now. I'm looking out of a different window upon life and death, with much more serenity and peace of mind; and I no longer take a tragic, darkly emotional view of the world, but a sort of comedy view.'

The dark realities of life have traditionally been the staple stuff of fiction – of the finest fiction, indeed. But when a novelist begins, like Rosamond Lehmann, to see a larger light, such realities begin to seem more like shadows: even to disappear into the light. And it is harder to write about *light*. Yet in this novel – which she does not intend to be her last, though it is her last to date – Rosamond Lehmann begins the attempt.

A Sea-Grape Tree is a story of movement, progress, and hope. It is also – like all Rosamond Lehmann's novels – a story of love. In it she rediscovers the life of a character we have met elsewhere in her work, whom she admits to be the closest in all her fiction to herself. We have glimpsed Rebecca Landon in Rosamond Lehmann's early short stories, lapped in the pleasant haven of her own childhood: a world rich in security and comfort, its luxury of calm enlivened by holidays and jokes and the odd intriguing acquaintance. In an earlier novel, *The Ballad and the Source*, we have seen this tranquility shaken, as Rebecca grows into adolescence in the first years of the First World War, and experiences – at a remove, but acutely, as is her nature – the extraordinary account of passion and drama with which her elderly neighbour and friend, Sibyl Jardine, regales her. And now, in this novel, we find Rebecca again.

She is changed: as everything around her is changed. A world devastated by one excruciating war is under the deep shadow of another. 'The heart of the world is broken,' says Ellie Cunningham; and so is our beloved Rebecca's, ravaged by the sudden betrayal that has ended a long flawed love affair. And Rebecca Landon is first and last a lover. 'I used to think the main thing in everybody's life was love,' she cries at the end of the book, in mingled hope and despair. 'But it isn't: I found that out long ago. People can manage with only a pinch of it – if that....I literally can't. I *cannot* live without love: without – you know, being in a state of love. A loved and loving state....'

2

Rebecca was to have begun a new life with her lover, making a voyage to a paradisal island in the West Indies. She embarked on that journey alone. Yet the departure she has made is at least as profound as she had intended; and she has arrived – in all her misery – at a place of hope. In a world of death, this island is alive with warmth and light: a place where love is possible and even present. Here the strangers can be healers – though the healers are not always strangers.

When Rosamond Lehmann sat down to write this novel, she knew that Rebecca Landon would be at its centre. She did not anticipate that on this Caribbean island Rebecca Landon would disinter another character from her own and her author's past. Literary creation is for this writer essentially an unconscious and involuntary process, in which she is almost as much of a spectator as her reader: waiting and watching as her characters emerge, develop, and move into unimaginable relationships.

For years after she had finished *The Ballad and the Source* (1944), Rosamond Lehmann had found that Sibyl Jardine, its complex and indomitable heroine, would not rest in peace within its covers; and she refused to leave her author in peace, as well. 'I just went on feeling: I must find out how this woman dies.' Thirty years later, she came to explore (as a writer) a group of people washed up on a Caribbean island, which she had herself visited long before: 'and I suddenly realised, "This is where Mrs Jardine comes to end her life."'

Sibyl Jardine has died before Rebecca Landon comes to this island. The fact does not prevent Mrs Jardine from disturbing Rebecca's solitude at a crucial moment in her time there, and engaging her in a characteristically sibyl-line conversation. This nocturnal visit is the only para-normal happening in the novel. Yet Mrs Jardine inhabits its world from the beginning of the story to the end. A sense of some deeper dimension shimmers constantly around the edges of its visible and tangible reality, and there is an incorporeal quality in its most solid-bodied inhabitants. In their mortal shapes Mrs Cunningham and Miss Stay may

3

be voluble, comical: yet they are somehow more present when they are silent than when they are speaking, as if their essential nature has a grace and strength belied by the oddity and indignity of their outward forms. For in their practical way, they are attendant spirits. They nurture and protect. They are channels of goodness and love.

Sibyl Jardine is – inevitably – ahead of that game, too. She has already 'discarded' her body, and with it stripped off some of the 'perilous stuff' of her old character and life. To Sibyl Anstey – as she once was, and as she has become again – Sibyl Jardine has become 'rather shadowy', not very important, 'not wholly admirable'. The horrors and complexities of that mortal life, which she shared with Rebecca Landon at a less advanced stage of both their developments, have become merely 'dreams' to her.

Her transformation is still in train, however, as Rebecca feels to her cost. Sibyl Anstey is not yet purged of the wickedness that interlaced Sibyl Jardine's power. As the relationships of the new story unfold, the old impulses flow back into her heart and hand: she tightens her grip on her last and most glorious human possession. But it is without force: her own greater strength – and Rebecca's – defeats it. In a moment, there is a double triumph, and a double joy. The dark reality is gone: the light remains. The love between Rebecca Landon and Johnny heals them both, releases them both from Sibyl Anstey's less noble incarnation: and, it releases the old schemer, too. 'She's gone,' says Miss Stay. 'Bless her, that's one of us saved.'

The intimations of immortality in this novel are delicate, implicit. They are not strident: they do not shout. But it is impossible not to hear them.

For the reviewers who first received this novel they were nevertheless hard to take. Some twentieth-century taboos had a more rigorous hold on their orderly rank in 1976 than at this time, less than a decade later. There was another reason for the frigidity of their response to this novel, however, which was at least as important. *The Ballad and the Source* was in 1976 unavailable and largely forgotten: and if it is inadvisable to read this novel without the later one, it is impossible to attempt *A Sea-Grape Tree* before reading its predecessor. The two books are part of a single whole. (I will not say 'halves', because *A Sea-Grape Tree* should also have a sequel.)

We are more fortunate now. Both these books are newly in print. It is also possible that *A Sea-Grape Tree* may find, in this republication, a new reception and response. It is Rosamond Lehmann's belief that our civilisation is moving towards a greater awareness of the worlds of reality that lie beyond the boundaries of what we experience in our lives on earth. 'Our leaden age of materialism is dying,' she says. 'The mills of God grind very slowly. The horrors are polarising and getting worse. But the light is also bursting out all over – even though it is hard for us to see it.' It is to be hoped that this new edition of Rosamond Lehmann's tender late novel will be rewarded with recognition and encouragement. For there is in the characters of this story an almost-perceptible life still to be realised: there is in this writer a further story to write. Rosamond Lehmann's readers – and Rosamond Lehmann herself – want that life, that story, born into the light of this world.

Janet Watts, London, 1982

Every evening, before the hour of sunset, Princess, the young maidservant, starts to light the lamps in the hotel: oil lamps, long glass funnels enclosed in brass containers with handles. Taking one in either hand, swinging them to the rhythm of her languid barefoot gait, she goes down, down the steep spiralling rock path to Captain Cunningham's bungalow. As darkness falls she is enfolded in soft light, she becomes a lustrous image, a black Madonna with a golden aura, borne through waist-high hibiscus bushes by invisible bearers to the sea. Her black eyes catch a gleam; and moths and fireflies drift to the lamps and hover round her. Sometimes she has set some object or other nonchalantly upon her shapely astrakhan-capped head: a jug or a bowl for instance, or a roll of toilet paper, or the Cunninghams' clean laundry. Down she sails through the electric air, through the thrumming, whirring, susurrating world of tropic nightfall; taking these beautiful lamps to the Cunninghams to give extra light to their verandah and their bridge table. This mosquito-proof verandah, its wooden pillars wreathed with bougainvillea, jasmine, clematis and flowering vines, is the social focus of the bay. Every three weeks or thereabouts in the winter months one group of visitors arrives at, another departs from the modest Victorian guest house which crowns the bay: British travellers mostly – stoutly upholstered middle-aged couples from the Midlands; occasionally a pair of honeymooners. But now and then appears a solitary person, a retired colonel maybe, or a naval captain (bachelor? – widower?), spry, alert, with innocent ideas and courtly manners; or maybe a woman on her own with paints and brushes; or botanizing; or convalescing; and self-sufficient; or a few wild, unsteady, wincing, patiently cherished or tolerated alcoholics, apt to linger; or just now and then, and usually male, someone who, though carrying a UK passport, and often seen around, and not overtly disreputable, broken, discredited or ignominiously labelled, continues silently, unassumingly to declare – but who notices or hears? who knows why or when? who asks? who cares? – 'I have resigned'; and to generate the miasma of failure and of humiliation; thereby causing social discomfort: or would cause it anywhere but here.

All these, going concerns and otherwise, quite a cross-section as Miss Stay the manageress frequently declares, are shepherded, under her strong leadership, down to the Cunninghams' bungalow, to add to the number of those who have signed their Visitors' Book, frequently adding a grateful tribute, or an appropriate line or two of verse.

The island is one of the smallest in the Windward group, not at all fashionable. Up to this year, which is 1933, it has scarcely begun to emerge from a paradisal state. Birds, butterflies, flowers, shrubs, flowering trees, and creepers abound in immeasurable splendour, profusion, and variety. No snakes. Idyllic isle. Only the natives do not correspond.

Princess is a physical exception – a perfect specimen, like a sudden rose in bloom on a waste patch; and some of the young children have a tender animal charm. But mostly they grow up undernourished, degenerate, vacant. The old sit slumped on the doorstep of their wretched shanties, smoking clay pipes, sunk in primeval lethargy. The more able-bodied, men and women, work in young Mr de Pas's plantation on the hill. They come down at sunset with their baskets and cutlasses, striding swiftly, not smiling when they pass a white-skinned visitor but

7

staring, staring and muttering in their throats. Once though, so Mrs Cunningham recounts, a young English woman, wandering alone (not very wise) to gather tree orchids, had an unpleasant experience. She was wearing candy-striped beach pyjamas – a garment never before encountered in these parts. When the natives saw her they stopped dead, doubled up with laughter, howling ambiguous comments. Then the women made a rush, surrounded her, fingering and patting her, half jeering, half admiring. 'What a belle! Oh, what a belle!' they cried. One of them snatched her beads and one her bracelet. She was frightened: they seemed on the verge of mayhem, about to tear her clothes off. The men stood aside watching with expressionless faces.

Young Mr de Pas came crashing round the bend of the hill in his antediluvian Ford, straight into the midst of them, honking his horn and braking with a blood-curdling screech. They scattered; in silence they sloped off down the hill. You would have thought he would have offered her a lift; but he passed on, not moving a muscle of his face. Not very chivalrous – but you have to get to know his funny ways. Queer chappie; lonely; you have to make allowances.

Whoever you are, no matter how recently introduced, you are urged, urged by Mrs Cunningham to stay a little longer. It is pleasant to relax in a rocking chair on the verandah and watch the sunset burn out from flame to rose to primrose and unearthly green on the horizon; to be fanned by the off-shore breath of wind that comes with the last of light. Also, far out beyond the towering palm-feathered bastions that enfold the bay you can watch the reef, watch the leaping ghost forever signalling, vanishing, as the wave forever breaks on it. Superstitious natives fear this beckoning spectre. Captain Cunningham, who is a splendid handyman, has cut back the bamboos, oleanders, tree-ferns in front of his abode to make a sizeable window; so that if he has a mind to he can train his binoculars upon the beach and spot any funny business that might be going on – anybody monkeying with other people's property: for instance, anybody making off with young Mr de Pas's motor boat, which is anchored in the bay; which the Captain borrows (with permission) when the fancy takes him to go fishing, or to drop in on a fellow he knows the other side of the headland. More often though he just sits on the verandah and keeps a sharp look-out.

'But would anybody?' asked the visitor: anonymous female person, with a discarded self, sitting between Captain and Mrs Cunningham, pressed, though delicately, to establish an identity, tense with the effort at all costs to conceal it.

'Would anybody what?' enquired the Captain brusquely; though perhaps not meaning to sound rude.

'Well, steal . . . make off, you said, with . . .'

'My dear Madam,' his stare flickered over her ferociously; though here again it might be merely the effect of eyes both prominent and bloodshot-blue, 'this isn't Paradise before the Fall y'know. They're born thieves all of 'em in these parts. Don't know the meaning of honesty. No use trying to teach 'em any different.'

'Do be careful, dear, to lock up any valuables,' said Mrs Cunningham. 'I'm sure you've got lots of pretty things, cosmetics as well – anything in that line the girls will take – scent or face cream or lipstick or even nail varnish.'

'Princess did ask me for my talcum powder this morning.'

'Oh, she's a naughty girl, she really is – we've all tried so hard to teach her better. I hope you said certainly *not*.'

'Well, no . . . I gave it to her. She said it was to powder her baby.'

9

'Oh, she is a bad bad girl! She's only just turned twenty and she's got *three* babies. I don't know who looks after them – her poor old granny I expect.'

'She told me she didn't fancy marriage, her husband might beat her, she said.'

'What she needs, the brazen hussy!' cried the Captain with enthusiasm; and his wife added, a thought swiftly: 'They don't go in for weddings much in these parts. Except just now and then, when they pass round the hat for a party. Then a whole bunch of them – all ages – pair off and the party goes on for days. By the way dear if you've got a camera be careful: they'll never leave you alone.'

'I'd like to photograph Princess. She's such a beauty.'

'A beauty? Hach! Ah well, tastes differ. Can't say she appeals to me.' He shot her a glance of furious distrust, seized his rum punch and throwing his head back took a long pull at it. Hoping to propitiate him, the visitor said hurriedly:

'What I meant about stealing . . . I thought they – the natives – rather avoided the beach. After dark anyway. The house boy, the one called Deshabille, looked scared stiff yesterday when Miss Stay told him to go down with a message for – for whoever lives in the hut on the beach. He wouldn't. Miss Stay had to go herself.'

'And Deshabille's such an obliging boy as a rule,' commented Mrs Cunningham. 'Oh, they're sure the beach is haunted. Staycie would bear that out.'

She turned for corroboration to Miss Stay, supine in a rocking chair behind her. But the manageress, her sinewy prehensile arms hugging her bony chest, her shingle cap askew, was sunk in deepest slumber.

'Oh ho, the duppies! Hach hach hach!' The Captain's mirth produced a series of loud hollow barking sounds. He raised his binoculars and raked the circumference of the bay.

'My dearly beloved spouse does not hold with ghosts,' piped Mrs Cunningham. 'He wouldn't even if he saw one. But I believe in them – oh yes, I do indeed. Some people are born psychic. Mummy was very psychic. So was my Highland granny. Second sight was second nature to them. And of course Staycie has the gift. She's a seventh child, you know. Are you psychic at all, Miss . . . ?'

'Care to have a squint?' To put an end to foolish prattle the Captain handed the visitor his binoculars, and watched her sharply while she fumbled with the instrument. Managing at last to focus on the beach, she trapped the double image: a hut, a sea-grape tree.

Stereoscopically vivid in the powerful lens, the sea-grape tree reared up, its pale trunk twisting smooth and serpentine, its branches carrying a canopy of glaucous blue-fleshed leaves and pendant clusters of green berries, sterile and hard as stone. Beneath the tree the hut: a sort of *cottage orné*, set up on stilts, with a high-pitched roof of rosy shingles, its walls stuccoed a deep shade of tawny pink; ornamented with shell encrustations: silvered-bronze shells, pearl, honey-coloured, milky flushed with rose and violet; shells of all shapes and sizes in convoluted patterns. A clumsy tarred old rowing boat was pulled up close to the front step, its oars propped against the tree. In the lambent twilight between lingering end of sunset and rise of the full moon every detail was still sharply defined. The close of day suffused the images in a dramatic darkly rose-gold light, defining every detail. Next moment all was blotted out. A long low whistle, an owl's hoot twice repeated floated up from the direction of the hut. Who was the inhabitant?

'That will be Johnny,' exclaimed Mrs Cunningham on a note of triumph. 'I always wait for it. Then I know everything's tickety boo down there. Louis will come now and row him out for his evening dip. There's a comfort in routine, don't you think, Mrs? . . . especially if you have to lie there day in day out like Johnny.'

'Doesn't have to,' growled the Captain. 'Got a very jolly bungalow, you can see it opposite, half-way up the hill. Every convenience. Stays down there for choice. Rotten luck on his wife.'

'Oh, he's married . . .'

'Yes. Well,' said Mrs Cunningham, with caution. 'Oh well, you can understand it, can't you? Swimming keeps him fit – and the hut's so much more handy. Louis is our boatman. He's as strong as an ox: he can carry Johnny as if he was a little child.'

'Can't he walk at all?'

'Paralysed from the waist down dear. The war. Oh, Jackie doesn't mind being on her own, I fancy! She goes her own way . . . and Johnny's grown to be more and more of a recluse. Morning and evening Louis rows him out and helps him roll into the water and then he swims and swims. Can't you imagine what it means to him, the freedom? – tearing through the water like a seal? I do believe he could swim for miles with those huge shoulder muscles and splendid arms of his. But Louis keeps within hailing distance, just in case. He'd lay down his life for Johnny. Poor old Louis, he's getting on. Some say he's a hundred, but of course he can't be. I do sometimes wonder – ' She broke off, looking mournful.

'Hach!' The Captain took another swig. 'All getting long in the tooth, if you ask me. Still, never know your luck. Keep yourself in trim, m'dear. Work those biceps up. Dumb bells every morning.'

'Don't be silly, Harold. It's a tragedy, Mrs . . . if ever there was one. Such a handsome chap he must have been, gorgeous! – well even now . . . He puts me in mind of Gary Cooper . . . you'll see for yourself. He was one of our ace pilots – a real dare devil. He crashed on a test flight behind our lines in France and broke his back – in the very last month of the war or thereabouts.'

'Rotten luck,' conceded the Captain glumly.

Though not glamorous, he too, with his stiff leg and bronchial wheeze was probably a war hero.

'Jackie was his nurse in hospital, and in the end she married him. I nearly said she caught him – though I suppose some might say he wasn't much of a catch, poor Johnny. Still, quite a step up for her socially, her background's very different, he comes from landed gentry, north country I believe. We always thought it couldn't have been a love match – I *knew* it couldn't. A man like that, such a proud chap, would never have borne to feel himself a burden to a truly loved one. I dare say it seemed the best solution.'

'Plucky of her,' muttered the Captain. 'Give her credit.'

He seized his walking stick and struck the floor a volley of violent blows; at the same time shouting to a tough-coated preoccupied looking mongrel terrier on the step of the verandah: 'Bob! Leave yourself alone, Sir! Have you got fleas or what's your trouble?'

The dog shot him a look of blank affront, described a half turn, and continued his investigations, his back towards his master.

'Now you've hurt his feelings. Poor Bobby, he can't help scratching, he's itchy all over. It's time you gave him a bath. Bobby's a somewhat morbid dog, Mrs . . . , He broods and he broods. He brightens up if you throw sticks for him but don't start it, he'd never let you rest.'

The visitor surprised herself by breaking into laughter.

'We all get morbid here,' continued her hostess. She sighed. 'It's the climate. It's a most enervating climate.'

'Have you lived here long?'

'Since nineteen twenty-two. We were the first white settlers, weren't we Harold – in a manner of speaking. There were one or two old Creole families, like the de Pases, going a long way back. But they've mostly died

13

out or left the island. Young Tony de Pas is the last of his line. Though I suppose he might marry . . . some nice strong healthy girl and . . . But somehow I don't – '

'Rotten bad life,' chipped in the Captain. 'Stands out a mile. Bad blood somewhere back along the line.'

'Too true, poor old Tony. There was a curse put on the family, so they say. I don't know why or when. We don't listen to gossip. Oh, but Tony's a scream. He ought to be on the Halls. He keeps us in fits with his imitations.'

'What does he imitate?'

'Animal noises chiefly – quite uncanny. He's a ventriloquist as well. He quite takes in poor Bobby when he throws his voice and barks from just behind him. He makes a rude noise and Bobby thinks it's him! Oh, and lots of other animals – birds too. You must meet him dear – he's a most versatile chappie. Oh, this' – she waved an arm widely – 'was one great flourishing estate once. You've noticed the old mill? Isn't it picturesque? The natives still tread the cocoa once in a while. But soon after the war our poor little island fell on bad days. There was a terrible hurricane, it stripped most of the plantations to the bone. The shock killed old Mr de Pas. Tony was just a boy then. He left school and set to and worked like a – well I mustn't say like a black, and got most of the land going again. That's when he put up part of it for sale. Harold saw it advertised and we came out on spec. The first guests at Invergarrie, weren't we Staycie? Oh, she's still snoozing. The old de Pas home that was, he turned it into a guest house. Those were happy times. We bought our plot and built to Harold's very own specifications.'

'How tremendously clever of you, Captain Cunningham. It is so charming.'

'Hach! Ah well . . . Suits our modest requirements pretty well. Show you over it one day.' He flashed a brief smile, more a twitch of the lips, in her direction. (Is he very shy, perhaps? – a sensitive, wincing man under the coarse exterior?) 'Not a palace. Fact is, m'wife thinks it pretty much of a come down.'

'Well, after Malaya, you know – that's where we were before the war. Waited on hand and foot! – we were spoilt I dare say. And then . . . it was lonely here at first. My husband is a very active man, he didn't take kindly to retirement, did you Harold? He can be very grumpy.' She cast a speculative eye in the direction of her unresponsive spouse. 'But then our little crowd started to come along – Jackie and Johnny – and a most interesting elderly lady, devoted to Johnny, she's dead now. And old Mr Bartholomew up at Invergarrie. He's Miss Stay's special pet. Now there's an interesting man. Such exquisite old-world manners. A great traveller, it seems; speaks six languages, very brainy.'

'Spouts poetry,' intervened the Captain.

'Oh, by the yard. He does let drop the strangest remarks. He's in love with his horse – Daisy her name is. He calls her his best girl, he *dotes*, my dear. Never a day passes but he's riding, riding, though he must be getting on for ninety, waving his hat and whooping like a cowboy, and talking to himself – or her, poor animal.'

'He sounds a little eccentric.'

'Oh yes, he is. If you want to study human nature, dear, you've come to the right spot. Then there's Kit and Trevor, the gay lads we call them. Dear boys, not boys exactly any more, very artistic and so kind and helpful. So we're quite a little colony. I only hope we can keep the atmosphere – well, *you* know, British. Oh, but I do miss England! How was it when you left? The weather?'

'It was snowing.'

'Oh *snowing*!' Her voice rose, lamenting and ecstatic. 'What wouldn't I give to see a white world again!'

'Burst pipes, what wouldn't she give for 'em.'

'Or one of those rainy soft spring evenings, the scent of wet lilac, thrushes and blackbirds singing their hearts out.

Real birdsong. There's a bird in these parts that gives me the pip, Mrs . . . Squeak, squeak, up and down, over and over on two awful piercing notes. Every blessed morning.'

'Not the brain fever bird, I hope?'

'Not *quite* so bad as that. The natives call it the day clean bird – cleaning the day you know – giving it a rub up. It's a picturesque thought.'

'Damn bird, I'd like to picturesque it. Innerkleen bird I call it.'

Such genuinely hearty chuckles shook the couple that, next moment, the rustle and creak of wickerwork signalled Miss Stay's return to consciousness. As if galvanised by an electric battery her face started to twitch throughout the layers of rouge and powder caking it. Next, one eye fell open, winked. Presently she exhaled a long tremolo of beatitude; murmured:

'Ah, what a treat to drop off after the long day's toil. A mor-or-ortal treat. Hark now!'

Violently she flung her head up; assumed the look of one intently listening.

In truth the throbs, brays, moans of a recorded dance band had begun to float from far across the bay.

'Jackie and her chums!' declared Miss Stay, exulting. 'They will be at it over there. Dancing and prancing! Prancing and dancing! – as the saying goes.'

'Jackie and young Tony get up little hops,' Mrs Cunningham explained. 'I fancy he's got a friend over from Trinidad, and one or two girls as well – nurses from the hospital. They seem full of go. You ought to join them dear. It's dull for you, sitting here with us – though we love to have you.'

'Oh no, no thank you, no,' cried the visitor appalled. 'I don't dance – I hardly ever . . . I love being here with you.'

'Jackie *lives* for dancing – she's taken up ballroom dancing. She and Tony went in for a competition a year or so ago in Georgetown. They got third prize. They're ever so skinny both of them, light on their toes. Strange when you think of it, him lying there, her swooping and twirling around just above him, so to speak.'

'Doesn't he . . . does he mind, do you think?'

'I really couldn't say,' remarked her hostess dreamily. 'Johnny's a dark horse, you never know what he's thinking. He never gives himself away.'

The visitor once more raised the binoculars and gazed at the shore penetrated now with the full moon's lambent pallor: the leaf-crown of the tree was rimmed with silver; the hut was a square patch of darkness. She strove to reach the person living silent and invisible within, who never gives himself away.

I will never give myself away.

Then the clock inside her head again; and then again the crepitation, recurring automatically, stringing her skull with red-hot wires. And on this verandah or inside her head, voices chattering, crooning, quacking: sounds without meaning, signifying nothing. Then all the sounds spun themselves together into a thick knot of toneless sound; which dissolved into a high-pitched humming reverberation; on which she was sucked out through a long tunnel into some kind of unfamiliar space. She was floating, bouncing a little, just above a strip of shore – the same shore, not the same: grainy, faintly iridescent, the tumbled rocks that ringed it insubstantial, moving like semi-fluid pools of bronze. The tiny shift of the waves crashed in her ears. And that old stranded reptilian-vegetable growth had lost its petrifaction, had come alive, was coiling down violently to earth itself, upward as violently into an explosion of undulating tentacles upon which floated a cargo of shimmering fruit and foliage. One great multi-fingered arm stretched across the hut, enfolding it in what seemed a tender gesture of protection.

Then suddenly, within this tent, with stereoscopic sharpness, the figure of a man appeared, standing as if in mid-air: naked to the waist, towering, edged with light from some source behind him. Primitive he looked, powerful, cold, with a fixed expression; like a ship's figurehead; or like a sea-god standing beneath a panoply made of those marine-fleshed leaves. Looking straight at her . . . through her? All at once he smiled, showing a mouthful of strong white teeth. The shock of this was piercing. It brought her back into her body with a bump. She looked round wildly, gasped out:

'*Oh!*'

The binoculars fell off her lap; were retrieved by her host with a glance of strong disapprobation. Gazing into a pocket mirror, reshaping her mauve lips a bright vermilion, Miss Stay was temporarily inattentive; but Mrs Cunningham enquired:

'What is it, dear? . . . Ah, you've seen Joey! Yes, there he is, that's our Joey, our lizzy-boy, our tame lizard.'

Sure enough, something vivid, sinuous, emerald, streaked along the balustrade, ran up a vine-wreathed pillar and froze there, only its throat pulsating.

'A lizard!' she said stupidly.

'Did he startle you? Isn't he a poppet? He's come specially to have a look at you – he always does when we have company. He's such a nosy boy. He lives up there, under the roof. The other day Harold put his hand out, and we held our breath, and he scuttled on to it, right up his arm and rested on his shoulder. It's quite uncanny how he watches us. Staycie calls him our familiar.'

'Our visitor will soon become acquainted with our local fauna,' declared Miss Stay, nodding and winking vehemently. 'Not to speak of our flora. This island is a paradise for nature-lovers. I daresay our visitor is a botanist and would put us all to shame with her lore.'

'Oh *no*!' protested the visitor, repudiating in the manageress a questing note, as of one bent, though delicately, upon a probe. 'I'm entirely ignorant. I've only just learnt . . . bougainvillea . . . frangipani . . . the trumpet tree . . . the flamboyant . . . the entrance flower . . .'

'The *what*?' barked the Captain.

'A climbing plant with a marvellous bell-shaped flower. It was all round the porch of the Inn where Deshabille picked me up. I asked him its name and he said: "Oh, dat is de flower of de entrance of de house. We call it de entrance flower. And dat dere is a common bird. On dis island we have no expensive birdies runnin' wild."'

Laughter rang out; Miss Stay exclaimed that that boy was a mortal caution.

Saved, I am saved, she told herself; hauled out in the nick of time, able to amuse and to partake in cheerful trivial conversation. Not the final crack-up after all. Merge yourself in flora and fauna, excellent therapy: for instance, identify with Joey. She observed the lizard who had now descended half-way down the pillar and was watching her, she thought. For a second she managed to change places: she was Joey on the pillar, motionless, indifferent, observing human specimens with a lizard's microscopic cold, intent percipience.

She dared now to tackle the binoculars again and see what could be seen afar by moon and starlight. Look straight into the dead centre . . . No longer dead. Light streamed steadily outwards from the hut.

Next moment, clearly seeing two figures move out and stand within the doorway, she hastily returned the glasses to her host, who exclaimed:

'Now what? Seen a duppy?'

He was irritated by her nervy ways.

'No. But it seems like spying.' Apologetically she added: 'I thought I saw him – the man – Johnny. I didn't know he could stand.'

'Ah well . . . Louis would be supporting him.' Mrs Cunningham had reverted to the dreamy note. 'The fact is he keeps it to himself what he can do, what he can't. He may surprise us all one day.'

'He will, he will!' cried Miss Stay in fervent affirmation. 'That blessed patient long-suffering fellow will rise up one day and walk towards us. Take up his bed and walk! I pray for it. More things are wrought by prayer . . . How did the poet put it?'

'I believe in miracles. My spouse does not,' said Mrs Cunningham, shaking out the hem of her skirt to fall just so, examining one neat ankle and pretty plump little foot in a white high-heeled sandal. 'All my life I've told myself: every day, every hour of every day, somewhere in the world a miracle is happening. God is showing himself to someone. Mummy taught me that, and I know it's true. Only we're so blind. Watch and wait. Expect but don't expect, she said.'

'Your mother was a wonderful woman, God rest her soul, no doubt of that.'

'She was. And we were all in all to one another. Some might say I was spoilt.'

'Privileged, not spoilt.' Miss Stay's nods grew more emphatic. 'And the privilege *not* one-sided, some might say, with such a daughter!'

Hypnotised by the voices' rhythmical monotony the visitor sank by degrees into a state of semi-somnolence. All bearings lost. Let them go. In the irrational element immerse. She let her hand move almost imperceptibly back and forth over her lap, rapidly scribbling on an imaginary pad. *Are they all mad?* it wrote. *The things they say! Is it the enervating climate? Are you dead drunk my dear? Captain, unbeliever, spouse, behold I will show you a mystery. A few moments ago sitting here beside you sipping one of your rum punches extra special brew I was cleft in two. My body stayed here dressed in pale blue-green shantung, I ME I was on the beach. Good God my dear. Very very very strange Madam!!! But it's true, very very strange but true. Everything but everything had stopped being solid was made of iridescent rays in webs and patterns that tree had come alive I saw its nature then I saw a MAN he smiled — did he see me? I don't think so the shock I came back with a bump and here I sit. Captain, a miracle has been vouchsafed. Perhaps I died for a moment. Another time perhaps for longer and never come back. This won't do now, wake up, pay attention to your hostess . . .*

Miss Stay was saying:

'My mother was a beauty. It was a mortal treat to see her dressed for the ball or it might be the opera. How she came to bring forth such an object as yours truly is one of life's enigmas. But she made the best of it! I never lacked for maternal love. "Now Clemmie never forget you have your own appeal" she'd say. As Ellie mentioned I was a seventh child. All the rest stillborn or died young. *Povera Mama mia!* The only one to reach maturity was little Clementina. The last of the line. Just a skinny ginger now. Just a stringy featherless old fowl.'

'Hey Hey Hey! Cheer up, old dear!' shouted the Captain. 'Never say die! Tell me your past I'll tell you mine I don't think! There's life in the old dog yet y'know! Plenty of *staying* power!'

'Oh Harold, what a *shocking* pun. Don't mind him Staycie dear, he's in one of his naughty moods.'

'Aha?' cried Miss Stay in strong appreciation. 'A joke! What a mortal treat it is to be among dearest chums and pass the joke around! And I know the Captain! He would never take advantage of a woman's thoughtless word. He's the perfect gentleman for all his wicked ways.'

'Take advantage? — never! Pure in thought word and deed — that's me!'

'And we are past all that, are we not, Captain dear? Casting sheep's eyes . . . canoodling in the moonlight. All our youthful peccadilloes, all behind us. No more beaux for Miss Clementina. Just an old stay-at-home, that's what she is, contented with her lot.'

'What what? Another pun? Didn't you hear my lady wife? Punning strictly forbidden on these premises.'

'Oh, and it slipped off my tongue quite unawares!' marvelled Miss Stay. 'It's a shame I do declare to be taken up so quick. And it was nothing but a case of tit for tat.'

'Let you off lightly this time. Shilling in the collecting box, Temperance mission to sailors. Come on, come on!' He extended a puffy hirsute paw with a tremor in it.

'I'm sorry to tell you, Mrs . . . ' said Mrs Cunningham gracefully lighting a cigarette, 'my spouse has somewhat of the bully in him. If you had had the misfortune to be married to such a brute for over twenty years you would know better than to try anything in the nature of – well, tit for tat. That would never answer. His ideal is the slave woman.'

'That's right! Give 'em stick! They thrive on it.'

'Will you listen to the man? Fawning – crawling on hands and knees – that is his notion of a woman's place. Ladies, are we to take it lying down?'

'Abser-lutely! Ver-ry nicely put! Ask nothing better! Hach hach hach!'

Miss Stay collapsed, gripping her bowed head in both horny hands, uttering moans expressive of mingled protest and delight. Perhaps acknowledging a limit to permitted badinage, the Captain heaved himself up and seized his walking stick.

'Ah well! Time for my constitutional. Just chunter along to the store – stocks need replenishing I fancy. So long girls, chin chin! Don't get into mischief. Any bridge tonight?'

Not waiting for an answer, he took a large canvas bag from a peg on the wall, whistled to his dog, went limping down the verandah steps and disappeared.

'Don't be late. Supper will spoil,' his wife called after him; adding after a moment: 'He won't have heard. He's getting very deaf.' She sighed. 'It's a problem how to tempt his appetite. He simply *pecks*. You wouldn't credit it in such a powerful build of man. It's the drink, I fear me. Would you call him a very heavy drinker, Staycie?'

Miss Stay gave herself pause before declaring upon a note compounded of the staunch and the judicial: 'I would say the Captain is partial to his drink. Exceptionally partial. But never have I seen him what you might truly call the worse. Never! What that man can put down while keeping on his legs is a mortal marvel. Sometimes with a drinking man the liver takes its toll. My own dear father succumbed – oh dear dear dear! Mark my words, Ellie, drink will never get the better of the Captain. All honour to you for your care of him. All the same, the man must be blessed with a champion specimen of liver.'

'Well . . . I keep out of his way some mornings,' objected Mrs Cunningham, smoothing away a little frown with the tips of her plump tapering fingers. 'He's a bit on the morose side.'

'Take no notice!' cried her friend. 'The man's leg might be playing him up dear, remember that. No – by and large, I do declare, if it came to matrimony I would never boggle at a drinking man. There's a masculine appeal . . . What says our visitor? Would she agree?'

'Well . . . I haven't much experience of – of drinking men. They can be a bit – a bit boring, don't you think? They repeat themselves . . . or want to quarrel, or . . .'

'Ah, when the dividing line is crossed! – that is another story.' Spasmodic twitches registered her sense of the need for delicate discrimination. Gazing towards the shore, Ellie murmured, as one speaking on the verge of sleep:

'Oh, I take no notice. That's married life, isn't it? –

give and take. His leg does play him up. I wish he had more to occupy his mind – he gets so restless. But men are restless aren't they? – more so than women. It's their nature.'

'Ah, women are the givers, that's the way of it. They were created to apply the balm.'

'Well, not always they don't.' A light mischievous chuckle issued from the throat of Mrs Cunningham. 'I do rub him up the wrong way now and then. On purpose.'

'A calculated risk!' declared Miss Stay.

'He's somewhat primitive.' The chuckle came again. 'I often recall what Mummy said to me when we got engaged. "Well Ellie," she said, "you are taking on a man with hidden depths. He's a man to put the woman he has chosen on a pedestal. Should she topple off she'd rue the day."'

'Oh, you'd never do that dear! Never!'

'Well, I'd never be a doormat. He knew that from the beginning.'

'The man worships you.'

Still reminiscent, Mrs Cunningham continued:

'I was a flirt, I must confess. I *could not* make my mind up.'

'So many admirers!'

'Ah well . . . Everyone spoilt me. And with Harold there was the age difference. But Mummy thought that was all to the good. You see,' – addressing the visitor – 'she kept it from me but she knew her days were numbered. She wanted to see me settled.'

'Security for her one ewe lamb!'

'Oh, security? Sometimes I wonder about security – where is it? The more we seek it the more . . . But yes, that was her idea. So we had a very quiet wedding. And afterwards she said with such a smile: "Now Ellie, remember, when the Call comes I'm ready."' Her face worked, her voice failed, went on shakily: 'That was the

24

first hint, to prepare me, but I didn't take it in. Harold knew, she'd told him, but he'd promised her not to break it to me suddenly. He simply adored Mummy . . . and we shared the nursing right to the very end. Three months and she was gone. He was wonderful, I will say. Of course she's very often with me – oh! very often. I tell it by the perfume she leaves – white roses, her favourites. And I sometimes think her going when she did was for the best. It would have grieved her when no grandchild came along. Believe it or not, Mrs . . . I haven't a single relative in the wide wide world, apart from a second cousin somewhere. It's the same on Harold's side. We're a pair of lone lorn orphans.' After a pause she added: 'Not that Harold ever wanted children.'

'Oh, as to that dear you must not repine. It was God's will for you in this life.'

'Oh, no doubt it was meant. I was delicate as a girl. Harold said from the first he'd never let me risk it. And starting married life out East . . . Oh, that was such a jolly life! Waited on hand and foot – so much going on, such a cheery crowd, always someone dropping in, dances galore, theatricals . . . I had some lovely friends. The war put paid to that gay life, of course. Harold threw up his job, he was getting to the top, and back we came. We both did our bit. After he went out to France in the REs I worked in a canteen, all through. It was hard, but there were some jolly times, so much *esprit de corps*. I daresay you were still in the schoolroom Mrs . . . '

Her voice ran down, she yawned, lapsed into silence. The rocking chair creaked, creaked. The visitor's hand started again to make scarcely perceptible movements on her lap, simulating rapid writing. *Now now steady on,* wrote the hand, *come come keep smiling smile awhile this is called free association very therapeutic. What on earth is going on where am I who are they??? Come come no crying now take a deep breath it'll all come right I am so lonely nonsense nonsense*

25

stick to facts observe surroundings observe Miss Stay she's made of clay dried clay and wire she wears a shingle cap pink silk net with strings tied beneath her scrawny chin why does she does she never take it off is it functional to tether a wig perhaps is it a wig such a curious colour or is it meant to add the final piquant touch??? I made one observation on the boat elderly people look a sad sad sight asleep puffing their lips out sagging so down in the mouth down and out done for LOST PROPERTY NO ONE WILL EVER CLAIM IT now stop that don't be like Bobby morbid think about lovely sleep sleep that knits up the ravelled sleep and forgetting forgetting think about children asleep — at home in their sleep drowned fathoms deep exposed and safe like fruit and flowers under glass think about water lilies on dark water now folds the lily think of moss-feather cocooning birds' nests think of chestnuts cream-dappled golden-brown moulded firm into hard green caskets lined with whitest softest spun silk substance DELICIOUS SIGHT that's better hold on to that dwell on things beautiful indifferent that lizard now those palm trees tossing in the moonlight leaning all together mop heads edged with silver lifting falling . . . Those women are asleep I think not noticing me thank goodness shall I write my dream down no I can't let's see if I remember it. She closed her eyes. Her hand lay still. Last night's dream pieced itself together.

A vast seashore flashed open suddenly: abstract of loved, played-on shores of childhood, the tide far out, cobbles and shingle sloping to tawny sand with ripples in its surface, the light strange, sunless. A girl on a pony galloping from nowhere, a girl with long fair plaits, recognised but different; and the pony half-familiar. Riding, almost flying, with joyful expectation, to reach the sea. Then girl and pony vanish; there is no more buoyant riding, no more shining sea. A hateful shrubbery builds up before her, undergrowth choked with dull dusty spiny thick-fleshed plants and shrubs; everything parched, starving, thirsty. A voice calls: 'Look at the tree!' And there, all at once, in the midst of that poisoned vegetable obstruction the tree appears, tall, slender, delicate as in a Japanese print. Its crown breaks out in blossom, snowy, rose-flushed. It shoots a branch out, and on this branch a bird: a bird with a jewelled crest and iridescent feathers. A Bird of Paradise. A voice says: 'Love Bird!' She stretches out a hand. It bends its head and pecks with a cruel beak; vanishes. A voice says: 'This tree must be cut down. It's dead.' She cries out: 'No! No!' – starts up awake, in terror.

Appalled all over again, she opened her eyes, looked wildly round to find Miss Stay gazing at her from the depths of hooded eye-sockets and murmuring:

'It's a mortal treat to see a fair woman in this corner of the globe. I love to see a fair-skinned woman. Lovers galore on her travels, I'll be bound!'

'Wait till the gay lads see you!' cried Mrs Cunningham with a light laugh. 'Not that they're . . . but they do appreciate artistic types. Trevor will want to photograph you, as sure as eggs. And you'll be a treat for Johnny. Between you and I, Johnny is my dream lover. But you'll cut me out, I fear me.'

'Oh no . . . I'm not . . . you're quite wrong, I'm not . . . I haven't been feeling very well . . .'

Tears spurted uncontrollably, streamed down her face. Mrs Cunningham leaned forward and gently dabbed at them with a tiny lace-edged handkerchief.

'What a shame dear. I thought you seemed a wee bit down. Not that you look it. All she needs is making a bit of fuss of, doesn't she Staycie? We'll see to it you'll soon pick up.'

'Thank you. Very kind . . . I'm sorry to be so . . .'

'Say something, Staycie!' cried Mrs Cunningham surprisingly.

Miss Stay said nothing, but remained with her head sunk on her chest as if in meditation. Her curious contours seemed to alter, to become stilled, imposing. Presently

27

she shook her head dejectedly, uttered a deep sigh. In the ensuing silence something seemed to be concluded. The visitor wiped away the last of her tears and felt her throat unlock. Mrs Cunningham started to hum the dance tune that came floating, throbbing down from the hill across the bay; broke off to remark:

'That tune is packed with sex. It makes me feel quite funny.'

'Packed with sex it is!' agreed her friend with fervour. 'Ah, there'll be some canoodling going on up there, no doubt of that! There's a time to dance, a time to – a time for all things in God's blessèd world. But give me one of the old songs dear for personal choice. *Annie Laurie* now, or *Barbara Allen*. 'Twould be a mortal treat to hear your sweet true voice.'

But Mrs Cunningham stopped humming and said almost with indignation: 'No, Staycie, no. I've forgotten *all* my songs. I'm quite ashamed to hear myself. You may not credit it, my dear, but once upon a time I was urged, positively urged, to take up a professional career. Mr Barstow was all for it – Rex Barstow, my teacher, you may have heard of him. A musician to his finger tips and such a charming man. When I broke it to him I was getting married he went quite speechless. The veins in his forehead stood out – I was startled. He was a married man, getting on for fifty. I always felt somehow there wasn't much sympathy between his wife and him.'

Uncoordinated sounds broke from the lips of Miss Stay, acknowledging a strong man's struggle for self-mastery.

'Round fifty is a tricky age for men, so I believe,' continued Mrs Cunningham reflectively. 'They have their funny time. I do sometimes wonder was he partial? – or could I have made good on the concert platform? But Mummy wouldn't hear of it. She felt I'd never stand the strain.'

'Ah, as to that, a mother would know best. Instinct would be her guide. She would sense the weakness – '

'I was never *weak*.' Petulance gave an edge to Mrs Cunningham's voice.

'Oh, morals are not in question, dearie! My meaning is, she would sense that the good fairies round the cradle had not bestowed one gift – the stamina, you know – to cling to the top of the tree against all comers. Dear, it was all for the best.'

'Well, it was Fate,' decided Mrs Cunningham. 'Everything is Fate, I think, don't you?'

'And therefore for the best!'

'Oh Staycie you are silly sometimes!' exclaimed her friend. 'What about the Bad Fairy? Seems to me she pops up at every christening.'

'Ah, there's a deep thought! What a deep thought you have uttered, Ellie. To tangle the skein and set us to the unravelling. What would life be without the challenge of it? Take it from me, girls, take it from this old bag of bones fit for nothing but the jumble sale, all for the best should be our theme song. Our trials and tribulations are just our schooling time, just our opportunity to learn our lessons. Just the Divine Plan for us.'

After a pause Mrs Cunningham remarked on a brighter note that we shall know one day.

They went on rocking, rocking. The visitor tested with caution the new element of peace and forgetting in which she seemed suddenly to move. Presently, as if arrested by some invisible beam, she intercepted the eyes of Miss Stay, like sunken wells with a star in their veiled depths, dwelling on her as if from a great distance. A deep voice issuing from her throat pronounced:

'*Trust your unhappiness as you loved your happiness and great good will come to you and greater freedom.*'

Then Princess glided into view, murmuring unintelligibly; whereat Miss Stay came to, struck her forehead and exclaimed: 'My Ancient of Days awaits me! Not to speak of new arrivals shortly to appear. Ellie I declare you are a siren. Linger longer Lucy is your theme song. I must stop my ears and wend my weary way.'

With a violent stamp of her black plimsolls she shot from her chair, executed a military salute, covered the length of the verandah in three loping strides, and was gone.

Mrs Cunningham burst into merry laughter. 'She's forgotten all about you! You stay here, don't dream of moving. Between you and I, dear old Carlotta isn't the best of cooks: Staycie doesn't notice. I was so spoilt in the East myself, I shouldn't criticise. But if Mr Bartholomew saw you dining alone he'd be likely to invite you to join him. He's the soul of courtesy but he can be a wee bit difficult. Do keep me company. My lord and master won't be back till – there's no knowing when. My guess is he'll end up with Jackie and her crew. They make a fuss of him.'

A handbell vigorously swung resounded from above.

'That's Staycie, take no notice. Poor Staycie, poor old darling. Isn't she priceless? That woman is a treasure.'

'She keeps reminding me of someone . . .'

'Fancy that! I would have been inclined to suppose that Staycie was unique.'

'Something in her turns of phrase, the same sort of picturesque vocabulary.'

'How well you put it! Picturesque is the very word.'

'Someone called Auntie Mack.'

'Fancy! Your Auntie, was she?'

'No, no relation. I only saw her once. I was about eight or nine I think. I haven't thought of her for years. Once, one afternoon; but she made a great impression. She seemed not quite real, like a pantomime character: a sort of witch, but a kind unfrightening comic one. I imagine a child might be – startled by Miss Stay. But fascinated.'

30

'Anybody might be. Staycie's outward form is quite a handicap. Her reflexes have simply gone to pot. You've heard of St Vitus's Dance? – it's something of the sort, brought on by shock. There's some grisly skeletons in poor Staycie's cupboard: madness, suicide, heaven knows what. I've never liked to probe, and personal troubles are what she never mentions. She's a lesson to us all.'

'Yes, indeed.' Indeed yes. Never mention personal troubles. Pack up your skeletons and smile, smile, smile.

'I don't know if you realise she's Guided.'

'Guided?'

'By Spirit. Entirely guided by Spirit. By her Voices. She's spoken through – when people come to her in trouble. She's never got anything for me, but then I'm not in trouble. If I ever were, I'm sure she'd give me guidance. That was a Message she gave you just before she left, it wasn't Staycie speaking. I tell you in case you were a wee bit puzzled. I believe it's the one Voice only nowadays.' The visitor remaining speechless, her hostess chirruped on. 'About trusting you know, and better times to come. I couldn't help listening. I thought it was so helpful.'

'Oh yes, it was, I thought so too. I – '

'Don't worry dear, I'm not inquisitive, nor is Staycie. Likely as not she wasn't aware of what came through. But I can tell you've had a nasty knock. You must just look forward, like she said. Maybe it was meant, your coming to this lost corner of the world. *Don't* think me nosy but it does seem strange you turning up alone, a bonny lass like you. We do mostly get couples, one sort or another.'

Dragging up words from a once more stiffening throat, the visitor said:

'I didn't intend to come alone. But at the last minute I got a message – ' With a painful grin she added – 'Not Staycie's kind. A telegram. Delivered to my cabin.

31

"Change of plans." '

'Change of plans?'

'At the very last moment. We were going away together. He decided against it, I suppose, I don't know why, he didn't say . . . The shock was . . .'

'No explanation?'

'No. Just: "*Breakdown. Forgive. Will write.*" '

'Breakdown?'

'It's a word he uses when – when our plans go wrong. I've heard nothing since.'

Stunned silence for a full half minute; after which broken words and phrases, such as cad, brute, men are all the same, much better off without, a woman's pride . . . issued from her shocked and sympathetic hostess; who presently enquired:

'You aren't his wife, dear?'

'No, going to be. At least that was the idea. He's got a wife. He'd left her, more or less, before we met.'

'A married man, oh dear! Well, my advice is you forget him. He's not worth another thought. Playing fast and loose like that with two women – I dare say more than two.' This unwelcome thought, which had crossed the visitor's mind, caused her to flush darkly. 'Harold would say he ought to be horsewhipped. So he ought!'

'You're so kind. It's such a relief to talk to someone. On that nightmare boat I stayed in my cabin the first days. But when it got warmer I couldn't. So I stayed on deck in a long chair and pretended to be ill. But there was a Colonel on board, a widower, he was very persistent – '

'You mean he was attentive?'

'Very. It was just curiosity I think. He said I was enigmatic. In the end he proposed to me.'

'*Well*! Didn't that cheer you up?'

Remembering the Colonel's conversation and appearance she violently shook her head.

'Some would say it's the greatest honour a man can do

a woman. Still, if you couldn't fancy him . . .'

'I expect I ought to have been more grateful.'

Nonsense talk, schoolroom talk, Girl's Own Paper talk, out-moded code of chivalry and gentlemanly behaviour talk. But comforting. Let the cad appear and be horse-whipped – yes, by Harold. The image rose and a spasm of laughter shook her.

'Forgive me if I'm speaking out of turn dear, but I hope and trust you'll have nothing more to do with him, not if he comes crawling on bended knee, as no doubt he will.'

A moment's mad conviction seized her of Mrs Cunning-ham's exceptional wisdom and prophetic insight. With an effort she rejected it, saying, but on a more cheerful note:

'It doesn't seem somehow quite in character. Let's not talk about me any more. Tell me about Miss Stay – her Voices.'

'Her Voices, well . . . She keeps quiet about them, or people would flock to her from far and wide. Or on the contrary she says they would have her certified. Not so very long ago she'd have been burnt as a witch, you know, like Joan of Arc. As it is she's had to pay and pay: gifts of the Spirit always have to be paid for, so she says. She can *see* as well as hear, you know. We had oh! such a lovely boy, a bull terrier, Sammy his name was, short for Samson. He died peacefully of old age but we broke our hearts. He's buried down there among his favourite bushes, where he hid his bones. Staycie looked in some days later and she saw him come in as usual, looking so frisky and rejuvenated, and shove his old head into my lap as he always did, then settle down by Harold's chair. I believed her of course, it seemed only natural, but Harold nearly had a fit. He thought we were – well, worse than barmy, wicked – playing monkey tricks with that precious animal sleeping quietly in his grave – pretending to *raise* him, or something of the sort. Staycie got round him in the end, she always can, he does respect her. In fact I think in his heart of hearts he longs to *believe*. Staycie's so clever with his prejudices. You may be wondering from the way I talk why ever I married the man.'

'No, no, not at all. Why people marry is so . . . '

'Yes, isn't it? A mystery. Not like anything else.'

'Besides, prejudices make for variety in people. Your husband might be less interesting without his prejudices.'

'Oh, you think he's interesting, I *am* so glad. He's a nice man, but his moods do give me the pip sometimes. Some people he can*not* abide. Nothing will shake him once he's taken a scunner.'

'I do hope he'll manage to abide me.'

'Good gracious, I should think so! He loves a woman with style . . . though come to think of it, style doesn't always answer. A most distanguay woman turned up here, I think I told you, not long after we came out – what was her name? – it's on the tip of my tongue, I never remember names. Well, anyway – she was quite elderly, very frail, weak heart. In fact, she died here. She and Staycie struck up an intimate friendship. Harold *could not* be in the same room – like some people are about cats. She had strange eyes that seemed to stare right through you – that's what he couldn't stand. No wonder, I told him, with a murky aura such as his.'

'How did he take that?'

'Oh I can always coax him back into a good temper if I go too far. Or nearly always.' She chuckled. 'Marriage is nine-tenths habit, don't you think? I sometimes wonder, if Harold should pass on before me, how could I break myself of saying "we"? That's marriage in a nutshell.'

'Yes,' said the visitor faintly, thinking: that, in a nutshell, is not the love affair. When 'we' can be 'we' in private only, or only in certain social circumstances, girders are lacking to keep the erosions in time's structures sufficiently repaired; thinking also that if you go travelling,

34

you find the world choc a bloc with co-habitations no less improbable than the union of the Captain and his mate. Day after day, year after year, lasting a lifetime. Beloved wife, beloved husband, when the terminal, very sad and trying illness comes to be rounded off with due ceremony in the obituary column. Sensible dull faithful couples, mutually tolerant, without pitched-up expectations. This bird-witted, this faded pre-war girl with her musical comedy airs and graces, pretty, pert, chaste, provocative, would never be a candidate for bitter sexual dislocation.

Presently Mrs Cunningham yawned and said:

'I'm getting a bit peckish. What about you? I tell you what – let's run down and take pot luck with Johnny, shall we? Why don't we? I'd like you to meet him.'

'He may not want to meet me.'

'Oh yes, he's sure to. Any friend of mine he welcomes. I quite often pop down of an evening when I know Jackie's entertaining. Louis's a wonderful cook. Come on, let's hurry.'

Skirting the palm tree grove that fringed one side of the bay, they emerged upon the beach – upon that crescent of dazzling coral powder, sifted with sand, with pounded mother of pearl, scattered with black driftwood, with ribbons of dry parchment-coloured seaweed, with broken palm shells, crab shells, with papery slivers of bamboo and other brine-bleached shards and skeletons, all frozen beneath the moon's full incandescent eye. Presently they pause just clear of the water's filmy verge, where the last crystal shallows and blue-rinsed transparencies slide in, dissolve, spilling over and over again a whispered breath, a lacy ruffle. They look towards that striking image in the middle distance: a hut, a sea-grape tree, moulded and spectrally illumined, netted in hard, snaking, blue-black shadows; the whole complex standing out in stereoscopic relief, with that air it has already started to create of mystifying weight and meaning. At the heart of it glows the amber effulgence of a lit lamp.

The visitor removes her sandals, feels the soft furry tingle of midget waves expiring round her feet. The other lifts her head and calls a long high-pitched *coo-oo-ee*. Silence; then an owl's hoot answers. 'That's him,' she says. 'It means All Clear'; and they start to walk towards Johnny's improbable dwelling. 'It's not just anybody I'd introduce, but he'll take to you. You have repose. Noisy people are what he cannot bear – loud voices, horse play. That lot Jackie collects up there – he can't abide them. And Jackie's as jerky and restless as a puppet on a string. I've mentioned he's the love of my life – it's the truth. He doesn't love me back of course, but he puts up with me. He's very kind. As I said before, I *hope* I shan't be jealous.'

'Of course you won't be – what an absurd idea. Does he love Jackie?'

'I think he hates her. I shouldn't have said that, forget it. The fact is, I doubt if he loves anybody. Perhaps he did once upon a time, before he – I believe he was engaged and broke it off, after the crash. Poor girl, whoever it was. I imagine her one of those long-legged outdoor English blondes. Perhaps he did love that old Mrs – I'll remember her name in half a tick. She was old enough to be his grandmother, but – well, I don't know, she didn't act like one. I suppose she must have been a famm fatall – and with that sort old age doesn't mean they're on the shelf. They've got something different from ordinary common or garden sex appeal. The same of course goes for Johnny, in a different way. You'll see for yourself.'

Then they have arrived before the hut, whose shell-encrusted surface gleams and sparkles; beyond it, Johnny is to be seen in a wheel chair drawn up to a table upon which a chess-board is set out.

*

36

'Johnny,' she said, 'I've brought a new friend to see you. She arrived a few days ago.'

'Yes,' he said, looking straight at me, with a pleasant smile.

'I *still* haven't caught your name dear.'

I said: 'It doesn't matter. I don't much like my name.'

'But you can't just be anonymous, my dear.'

I was struggling with my neurotic compulsion to obliterate my identity, not to reveal my name, when he said gently:

'She can if she wants. She's travelling incog. We'll call her Anonyma.'

'Anemone! – that's pretty – Greek isn't it? It suits her, doesn't it, Johnny?' Poor Ellie, thrown by some element in this botched introduction – perhaps by the sense that his unexpected response seemed to establish some immediate link between us – began to lose her nerve and gabble.

'I promise,' I said, 'I'm not on the run from the law – or from anybody.'

'I'm delighted to meet you in any case,' he then said in a formal manner. He had a deep throaty voice, tinged with melancholy like all seductive voices. One could imagine him using it once upon a time to tease and to beckon and to keep at arm's length the women whom he fascinated.

'Excuse my not getting up,' he said, still looking at me, wheeling himself forward. I saw then that his knees were covered with something that looked like a light blue cloak. 'Come and sit down. But where?'

'On the step,' said Ellie sharply. 'Here's a cushion for you.' I thought once more that she was put out by this long exchange of looks, fulfilling, so it would appear, her worst suspicion: that love at first sight had taken place – or if not that, that she was telling herself: Really! to stand and stare, how rude. For it was he, all right, that I had seen earlier: dark hair, thick and wavy with a broad white lock in it, points of it sticking up on end, still damp from bathing and unbrushed; blue shirt open at the neck, tremendous shoulders; black, angled eyebrows, smile uncovering large regular white teeth and all. His eyes were long and light, the colour of clear sea water on a sunless day, and cold – yes, cold. His skin had a waxen look, with a stain of carmine over each prominent cheek-bone. This gave his dramatic face an extra touch of unreality – that sea-god, ship's prow look I had watched before.

We sat one on each side of him on the top step, looking out at the sea's great lustred semi-circle. Louis brought us rum punches; and later little grilled fishes with lemon, and platters of mixed fruits: pawpaws, bananas, avocado pears. Our tongues were loosed. Johnny drank steadily; perhaps we all did. Looking over my shoulder I saw a room lined all round with well-stocked bookshelves. There were bamboo screens; a gramophone; a guitar; a typewriter; a cane *chaise longue*.

At some stage in the evening Ellie persuaded him to show me a folio of line drawings washed with water colour: still lives of shells, leaves, orchids, lilies, fruits – all sorts of ravishing indigenous objects. They were charming. But when I said so, he said: 'Oh, rubbish,' and shut the folio. 'It was just a hobby.'

'You don't mean you've given it up? That's naughty,' Ellie exclaimed. 'You were going to make a book of them.'

'So Sibyl imagined. It was an absurd idea.'

'You and her together – a book about the island. She was an authoress, wasn't she?'

'Among other things.' His smile broadened, then abruptly faded.

'Anstey!' cried Ellie. 'It's just come back to me, Sibyl Anstey. You should have known her, shouldn't she Johnny? A most unusual person.'

'I did know her,' I said; but either they didn't hear or

38

I said it only half aloud. By that time my head was spinning.

He said reflectively, with a tinge of irony: 'She certainly kept us all up to scratch.'

'Oh, she did! Do you remember those – what was it? – spiritual exercises she taught us? – to release something or other. What was it she was always going on about?'

'Our untapped creative potential, I expect.' He laughed a little.

'Well, they didn't tap mine,' said Ellie, glum.

'You didn't try hard enough.'

'Or Jackie's, or Kit's, or Trevor's. I did try – she wasn't interested, except in tapping yours.'

'Ellie didn't really take to her,' explained Johnny.

'That's not true. I admired her so much. She had no use for me, why should she have? So brilliant and . . . Still, when people make you feel it, it's not very . . .' Her speech by now was blurred. A gush of tears spilled over and ran down unchecked, giving her moon-chalked face with its slightly protuberant round eyes and cupid's bow mouth a look half comic, half pathetic, like a woe-begone Pierrette.

I broke in saying: 'You mustn't be upset. It wouldn't have occurred to her, what you were feeling. She would have said: "I don't know how it is but there seems some kind of malaise between that charming woman and myself. What can be the cause? Could there possibly have been some failure on my part?"' I heard my own voice adopting more and more of remembered tones and inflections. 'Oh, and other things she would have said. Like: "You must educate your eyes to *see*. Learn to observe with *accuracy*. I can paint flowers very beautifully. So could others if they could only learn to notice the green in the white."'

They were both staring. Ellie looked awestruck; one of Johnny's eyebrows shot up sharply. I launched into my explanations. In a blinding flash I saw myself, with Jess and Mademoiselle, toiling up the goose girl hill with primrose baskets, opening a blue door in a high strawberry-brick wall, and for the first time confronting the Enchantress.

'I adored her,' I said. 'She told me long long stories, she bewitched me. She had three grandchildren, Malcolm, Maisie and Cherry. We used to play bicycling games in her garden. And climb; and swing. There was a Major, her husband. He never spoke: Major Jardine. She was called Mrs Jardine when I knew her. I remember, Anstey was her maiden name. Wasn't she called Mrs Jardine here?'

'I never heard her mention any Major of that name. Did you, Johnny?'

'Not often,' he said guardedly.

'Perhaps there'd been a tragedy in her life,' said Ellie, struck with a happy thought. 'She may have wanted to forget. This is a great place for – well, for leaving the past behind.' She shot me a part-conspiratorial part-apologetic glance.

'There were quite a few tragedies in her life,' I said. 'Dramas galore, from the days of my grandmother onward, from when she was a girl. The Major died during the war. He was a very sad silent man: what Miss Stay would call a drinking man, I realise, looking back. It couldn't have been easy, living with her. She used to correspond with my mother, but after the war we all lost touch. I wonder why she came here. *Pour le recueillement?* She used to talk of the necessity for that.'

'Yes, that was it,' said Johnny.

'She came because of you, Johnny,' said Ellie sharply. 'She followed you – you know she did.'

'I was in her hospital for months in France,' explained Johnny, stubbornly sticking to facts. 'We got to know one another fairly well. She was very good to me – helped me put myself together again. She had a gift for that. Occupational therapy, you know.'

'Basket weaving?' suggested Ellie.

He laughed. I said: 'She would be more original than that'; and he agreed. I saw their relationship in a sort of clouded flash: this beautiful stricken man; why she had followed him. Out of a cave of memory sounded again the dark harsh-tender siren notes of Mrs Jardine's voice proclaiming and lamenting her lost lovers.

'She died *here*?' I said. 'I can't believe it. When?'

'Not all that long ago – two years, wasn't it Johnny? She had a doctor granddaughter she was very proud of. Did you know her?'

'Maisie – oh yes! I didn't know she was a doctor.'

'Dr Maisie Thomson.' He sounded amused. 'Splendid person.'

'She was sent for – Staycie sent for her, I think. Anyway she was here at the last. But I never met her, such a pity. Harold took a fancy that year to go cruising round the Islands. When we got back it was all over. There's only one tiny church here, on top of a hill – that's where she is. I went once with Kit and Trevor to see her grave. Just SIBYL ANSTEY on the headstone, not even the dates. A little insipid for such a colourful personality, but her express wish, I gather, Johnny.'

'Yes.'

'Fancy you having known her, what a strange coincidence. It's a small world and no mistake. I suppose you've read her books?'

'No, never. They were banished from our library. Disapproved of. Very unpleasant books, my mother said.'

'Good gracious! Somehow I would have thought they would have been – romantic more. Idealistic. Were they on the frank side?'

'Trash, my father said. Somehow I suspect they may have been.' To intercept her reaction to this harsh opinion

41

I went on quickly: 'But Sibyl Anstey, Mrs Jardine – oh, she was like a legend! Mythical Queen. One doesn't forget such phenomenal persons, ever. I used often to dream of her.'

I hurried on with my reminiscences, playing them out as it might be on a length of rope to reach a group of human figures marooned in time past, myself among them. The element of something approaching the uncanny in this turn of events excited me and made my descriptions vivid, picturesque.

'What a happy childhood you must have had,' said Ellie. 'Those lovely homes and gardens. Such a happy family, so many playfellows. I was an only child and – well, pennies were scarce after Daddy passed away. Mummy couldn't give me all the opportunities she would have wished.' Another freshet of tears spilled over, and Johnny handed her his big clean handkerchief, saying kindly:

'Mop up, ducks. Wipe the tear baby dear from your eyeee'; at which she burst into weak giggles and exclaimed: 'Aren't I an idiot? It's your fault Johnny. I can't explain, but it is. Thank you for this gorgeous hankie, how good it smells, may I keep it?' She flung it over her face, inhaling deeply; then said with a sly peep in my direction: 'I *had* a dinky one, but it went west earlier this evening. *Soaked*, dear – wasn't it?'

I too was giggling now. I said: 'Yes. That was Johnny's fault too, I expect, though I can't think why.'

'It's the fault of the full moon,' said Johnny, 'according to Louis. If you feel like howling, that's the reason.'

'I can well believe it,' said Ellie, lifting her head accusingly towards the sky. 'Princess says the same. Never expose your face to it when it's at the full, and *look* at us! – absolutely plastered with it. Plastered is the word . . . I do feel very queer.' She stood up, not quite steadily. 'I must go. Harold may be waiting for me – *may* be.

Johnny dear, goodnight. You look like a handsome ogre in the moonlight, your teeth quite glitter.'

She ran a hand over the wall of the hut, lightly tracing out an ornate cluster of shells. 'All Sibyl Anstey's work, eh, Johnny? Well, I know you helped. And we all helped to collect them. Louis built this dinky little house for her, didn't he Johnny?'

'Yes, he did. And dinky it is *not*,' he snapped.

I said, to help her to recover: 'It's a work of art.'

'Yes, isn't it?' he said. 'You could call it a bijou residence, I suppose; but it's very solid and neatly designed inside.'

'Did she live here all the time?'

'No. She slept up aloft under Staycie's wing. But every day Louis would carry her down and carry her back again at night. She liked that.' He smiled with a downward look, spreading his hands out on his knees, smoothing the blue wrap that covered them. He had big useful hands with spatulate finger tips. It was then that I suddenly recognised the wrap.

Ellie said: 'Louis made her a sort of chair on stilts, didn't he Johnny? – for doing her shell work. She always seemed so busy, but the funny thing was she'd often lie for hours on her *chaise longue* just staring out to sea.'

'Busy all the same,' I said.

'Inside herself, you mean – busy with her thoughts. You could tell she was a deep thinker.'

'The arrangement is,' said Johnny, 'that this delightful dwelling is mine until Maisie claims it. I'm her tenant. What's more, the rent I pay is nil. Am I not lucky?'

'Will she come out?' I said, telling myself that nothing would surprise me now. Maisie might well appear, saying in her ironic way: 'Oh, so it's you again, Rebecca.' I conjured her up in a white overall, a stethoscope depending from her formidable bosom, calves bulging above sensible flat-heeled shoes: a square, highly-coloured figure with brilliant penetrating eyes.

'She might come one day,' he said. 'I hope so. But I doubt she'd spare the time. She's head of the gynaecological department in some hospital – somewhere in the north; and a private practice as well. She sends me postcards now and then.'

'And do you write back?' Ellie spoke severely.

'Of course.' He grinned.

'I wonder!' Addressing me, she continued: 'Her granny was so proud of her.'

Another random image flashed on me, this time recollected, not invented: Maisie with burning cheeks, her hair standing up on end like copper wire, tilting back her head to blow a pheasant's feather up, up, till it lodged in a bunch of mistletoe. In the huge kitchen, on Christmas Eve, 1916, in Mrs Jardine's desecrated house.

What I was being told seemed to follow naturally, logically from that night of our last meeting, despite the huge gap in time and space: a natural outcome but also phantasmagoric – even slightly sinister.

Johnny had now picked up his guitar, and was strumming on it in an absent way – giving us, I thought, our *congé*. As we finally moved away he glanced at me and said quietly:

'Come again.'

We walked off, not quite steadily, arm in arm; and when we came to the place where our paths diverged – hers through the grove of palms, mine to the steps cut in the rock – we stopped. Turning, she held out Johnny's handkerchief and waved it once, twice, in his direction. She murmured: 'Goodnight, my bonny love, God keep you.' Then she dropped her arm and said with a quaver: 'Well now you've met him. I knew he'd take to you.'

'I don't see why you think he did.'

'Oh, I can tell! For one thing, he asked you to come again.'

44

'That was just politeness because I was with you.'

'No it wasn't. He's never said it before. I expect you think I drop in on him any old time. I know I told you I did, but the fact is I don't. For one thing, Harold's not *all* that keen. He thinks Johnny unsettles me.' She fell into a brooding silence. 'Besides which, I can't get over my silly shyness when I'm with him. Till I've had a few drinks, and then I'm even sillier.'

'I'm sure he's very fond of you,' I said.

'Do you really think so? He can be so – not exactly snubbing. Keeping his distance.'

'That's just in self-defence. His way of coping with his – handicap.' It seemed to have become my turn to be the comforter.

'You may be right: in case anybody ever hints at pity. He's so proud. Oh, the cruelty of life sometimes!' She sat down on a rock, pressing his handkerchief to her face. 'I worship him. I have such wicked thoughts sometimes, such as, I'm almost *glad* he's like he is. Where would he be? What would he be doing? It doesn't bear thinking of – breaking women's hearts, letting them eat him up between times, I dare say. As things are, he's *grounded*.' She jumped up, shook her skirt out, but still made no move to leave me. 'I don't know what I'm saying, take no notice. We're all mad about him – Staycie, Louis, me . . . He doesn't love *us*, but we don't mind.'

'What about his wife?'

'Does she love him, you mean . . . Well, I must be charitable. She may have been hurt . . . I wonder. But she'd never let on. There's nothing *inside* her, if you know what I mean. She's like a tin – you shake it and something rattles – dried peas or something. Oh, she's quite friendly when we meet, she likes a joke. She comes down and has a swim sometimes. Or now and then when she's not swanning around with her chums and practising her tangos and things, we make up a four for bridge and have a pleasant evening. Harold sticks up for her: he says she's plucky and Johnny shows her no consideration. She's lost her job in a manner of speaking: Louis has completely taken over looking after Johnny. No one else is allowed to touch him. Louis would *die* for Johnny. He scarcely ever speaks, only sort of grunts out bits of words, and murmurs in his throat; but he understands Johnny's every mood and wish. He's got a gorgeous singing voice, has Louis. Deep, rich. Sometimes I hear him singing at night to the guitar – old plantation songs. Then I know they're happy. Still, the songs do sound sad.' She sat down again, plunged her head in her hands. 'Life is sad nowadays, Anemone. You may not agree with me, but there's been a *change*. August 1914 it started. Nothing will ever be the same. The heart of the world is broken. I said so once to Johnny and he said yes, and watch out for the next thing, people will be born without hearts and a damn good thing too. That's haunted me. It couldn't really happen, could it?'

I was dumb: such a possibility seemed too near the knuckle; and next moment, recalling my plight, she put an arm round me and hurried on: 'Of course it couldn't. He didn't mean it either. He was in a bad mood – he does get awfully blue, no wonder. I think he misses that Anstey woman. She did keep up his spirits – with her unusual outlook. What a personality! A bonny fighter, wasn't she? She fought for him. She was determined to get him on his feet again.'

'I can imagine it. That was always the pattern: to have someone in her life, a superman, that she could make into her own special superman.'

'Cure them, you mean, if they had something wrong?'

'Well, in a way.'

'By prayer, or laying on of hands or something?'

'No, no. By casting her spells. By the power of her will.'

Ellie reflected, then said severely: 'That could have

been against the will of God.'

I laughed. 'That wouldn't have bothered her.'

'She wasn't a Christian?'

'No. Well . . . she might have said so, and meant it, sometimes. But I think all her shrines were pagan.'

Ellie said, after a pause: 'You're clever, aren't you? I saw you were, at once.'

I said: 'I remember one of them very well – one of her supermen: a sculptor, from South Africa. He was killed. He was rather wonderful. He let her down though. They all did, one way or another.'

Ellie remained thoughtful. 'Johnny is wonderful,' she said presently, 'and he couldn't have left her, not under the circumstances, if that's what you mean by letting her down. He really was fond of her. After she died he seemed to get more apathetic. I used to hear them laughing together while they were playing chess or something. That was so nice.'

It occurred to me that in the old days I had never heard her laugh: had never connected her with laughter or the absence of it. In my childhood, the word would have conjured up giggling fits in the night nursery, *fou rire* in church or class; or else the daemonic sounds arising from the kitchen quarters, especially when gardeners dropped in for elevenses during their employers' absence: up-and-down-swooping shrieks, convulsions of agonised hilarity, interspersed with rumbling bass obligatos – the whole suggesting a world of mysterious and potent sexual innuendo.

But Ellie's kindly naïve words had evoked a particular intimacy, an irreplaceable pleasure, which I too had known and was deprived of now. For the first time I could imagine Mrs Jardine natural, her panache and her swank discarded, behaving like any woman happy with her lover, and sisterly towards other happy women.

It seemed somehow fitting when Ellie added compassionately: 'What a tragedy to lose that little grand-daughter. I wonder if Staycie helped her? I expect she did.'

I had not thought of Cherry, not consciously at least, for many years; or of any of the sufferers in that disaster. But now they were all astir again within me; and the experience, its actual nature, pierced me like a knife thrust. It is easy to dismiss what an undeveloped heart cannot imagine: brutal severance; lacerating self-reproach; pain without remedy, stoically endured. But I was older now; and Cherry, no longer a winged denizen of a land not open to strict scrutiny, came back sharply for a moment, sitting up in bed and reading aloud to Harry.

Ellie began to sing softly, in her husky voice:
'Poor Butter*fly*! – 'neath the *blos*-soms *wait*-ing,
Poor Butter*fly* . . . for she loved him so.
The *mo*-ments passed into *hours*,
The *hou*-ers passed into days,
And still she *sighed*:
The *moon* and I . . . know that *he'll* be *faith*-ful,
I *know* he'll *come* – to me by and by . . .'

She broke off, got up, said: 'That's quite enough. See you tomorrow dear. Drop in whenever you feel like it. You're always welcome. I think it's time I gave a little party. Be careful how you go. There's a great big bull-frog sits on the path sometimes – a lovely boy. Don't step on him. Night night.'

She stepped away briskly into the shadows. I sat on, listening, watching. Earth's myriad midget dynamos throbbed on, secretively, insistently. The gramophone no longer moaned and bawled. Cocks crowed at the moon, dogs barked and barked across the hills, through all the valleys. The tropic stars hung down so huge and low they seemed not altogether out of reach. I looked far out for the spectre of the reef; its demented twists and menacing

48

collapses had undergone a metamorphosis; had become a dance, inspired, elastic, rhythmical; as if some phantom god with streaming crystal locks were leaping in majesty, flinging out spangled veils to hide his presence and reveal it. The wind on the sea seemed to carry a faint sound, a shimmer as it were made audible, or whispering become light's essence. Or the laughter of disembodied creatures – Allegra beings, buoyant among the waves, clapping their hands for joy.

The lamp in the hut went out: Johnny had been put to bed. A tall figure could be seen to slip out, hang something on a branch of the sea-grape tree, come clear of its shadows, pushing the boat down to the water's edge. He waded out, got in, pulled on the oars and glided off. Louis, gone fishing.

I was part floating part anchored in a world without stain; purged of spells, charms, humans, duppies and all harmful things. My laceratingly unacceptable identity no longer troubled me; I was nothing but pure exhaustion, supreme astonishment: the trackless wilderness in which I had been stumbling had led me back to the door in the garden wall. Yet it seemed unreachable; and if Mrs Jardine was waiting behind it, it was for others, not for me. She had become a statue, a marble monument raised to imagination, industrious imagination, superimposed upon that idyll she had dreamed of – a life-style of arcadian simplicity: fruit for the picking, fish for the fishing, all the island for her garden, all the shores to comb for shells; dark-skinned primitives to serve her, worship her; and at the heart of it all, her treasure trove, her stranded Titan; the one, the unique, the corresponding inmate. As it was in the Golden Age.

> '*Sweet Lord, you play me false!*'
> '*My dearest Love, I would not for the world.*'

She was dead now, safe; and he still captive. They could not if they would . . .

All the same as I climbed up through the barrage of moths, fireflies, cicadas, and looked back a last time in the direction of the hut, I fancied a figure watching me.

Now and then, late at night, from the other side of the wood-panelled wall which divides the visitor's austere bedroom from the one next door, comes a medley of curious sounds: shuffling footsteps, mutterings interspersed with volleys of sharp slaps. It is Mr Bartholomew, goading his antique frame into activity, driven by the mindless automatic restlessness of extreme old age; or by the fear, perhaps, that if he lay down to sleep, death might pounce unawares.

But why from time to time does he rain smacking blows upon his skull? According to Miss Stay, when these sounds are described to her, it is his little device for driving out unwelcome thoughts: or possibly he is acting out cowboy fantasies of being a crack shot.

What he goes on muttering is poetry – a random anthology of lines and phrases culled from Shakespeare, Milton, Racine, Dante, Keats, Byron, Shelley, Wordsworth, to name but a few. He loses the thread, stamps, curses obscenely, starts again. Beneath the bridal swathes of her mosquito net she lies and listens, is sometimes tempted to yell a prompt line, more often tries to block her ears, or considers doing him violence. Finally, after a particularly prolonged bout of slaps, he is complained of by the couple on the further side. Miss Stay registers dismay but not surprise; explains that he does have these trying turns, agrees that it won't do, and banishes him to the annexe with Winkliff the garden boy for guardian. She does not permit him to move in with Daisy, as he would prefer. No no, he would not, she tells him in a scolding voice, give the poor animal a moment's rest; and heaven knows she earns it. He knows better than to argue; but come daybreak he is up and dressed and off, scampering over the rocks to Daisy's humble shack behind the cocoa mill. Leading her forth with endearments and caresses, he saddles her and mounts her. At a plodding pace she ambles out of sight with her bizarre burden; up the road that climbs to the plantations and beyond them to the island's heart: to grass abounding, says Miss Stay. Yes, yes, he leads her to sweet pastures. There, watched by her inamorato and shaded from the burning sun of noon, she relishes luscious revitalising provender. Often they do not return until the sunset hour, and heave into view at a fairly creditable turn of speed, Mr Bartholomew whooping and whirling his Panama hat in cowboy fashion. With a flourish, he dismounts; Daisy relapses into her customary drooping and apathetic stance.

Mr Bartholomew is a favourite with the female staff who, when the spirit moves them, plait him a splendid lei of orchids and hibiscus. At his insistence Daisy gets one too, and then – he is relentless and imperious – he calls for 'the photographer'. This is Kit, who never fails to oblige, and to present Mr Bartholomew with the results: though, as he cheerfully remarks, it could almost be called a waste of time and film, for Mr Bartholomew is all but blind and cannot, surely, descry his curious image – his gaunt, hobgoblin frame contained in a once elegant now frayed, discoloured suit of biscuit-coloured linen, several sizes too large for him; his skeletal head and wintry moth-eaten beard; his air of mingled intellectual distinction and decay incongruously posed against Daisy's dejected profile or indifferent rump. Sometimes his arm is flung about her neck; sometimes he is making as if to offer her a titbit; but always the effect is of a one-sided emotional relationship. And never does he display these records of his pastimes and obsessions: he flings them into a drawer, locks it and hides the key. If Miss Stay knows where he hides it, or what other clues to his identity and buried days are there secreted, she does not tell. Is he a bachelor? A widower? A once eminent professional or academic person now fugitive from life? or from the law? No letters come for him. When Miss Stay goes once a month to Port of Spain for (so she says) her beauty treatment, she cashes a sizeable cheque for him; and then he tips the staff with reckless prodigality, orders in cases of rum and whisky and throws a midnight party in the kitchen.

Johnny is carried up from the hut amid enthusiastic cheers on these occasions. The revels start in a spirit of old-world grace and courtesy. To the strains of Louis' accordion, Mr Bartholomew rotates with Miss Stay in a decorous valse, while the staff clap hands and give utterance to yelps and throaty snatches of musical encouragement. But within the hour, mayhem has broken loose; Miss Stay curtsies to Mr Bartholomew, kisses her hand to the assembly and retires; and the party drifts, reels, prances down to the shore and there continues with howls of laughter and general abandon. A huge fire of driftwood and dried palm shells is lit to banish any lurking duppy. Johnny is set down on the top step of his dwelling; drinking steadily, he alternates between strumming on his guitar and changing dance records on his gramophone. Kit and Trevor trip over from their bungalow to join him. They lend an air of cheery domesticity to his aloof and striking figure. When not attending him, they dart hither and thither through the party, bestowing greetings, hugs and kisses, collecting fuel for the bonfire, whisking the inebriated away from contact with the flames. The Cunninghams have appeared to join the fun. After a couple of drinks or so the Captain allows a mellow mood to take over, and needs little coaxing to render one or other or all of his three songs: wholesome, manly songs of bygone years. In a powerful if unmelodious bass he renders *The Floral Dance*; then *Uncle Tom Cobley*; finally a song whose rousing refrain rings incongruously upon these languorous shores.

Sing ho! sing hey! for merry merry mer-ree maids!
Their eyes are bright and glow-owing,
Their eyes are bright and glow-owing,
But what their way with a man will bee-ee-ee (Pause)
My goodness! My goodness! my goodness there's no KNOWING!

Stiffly, unsmilingly he bows, acknowledging applause; roars 'Put it down Sir!' as Bobby is seen to emerge from the shallows, a crab depending by one pincer from his lip; limps away without another word.

Mrs Cunningham remains. In Malaya, she says, we used to sing duets at all the local concerts; but no no no, nothing will induce her to sing in public any more. However, she enters into the party mood and dances quite a provocative tango with Kit and Trevor before going to sit at Johnny's feet. He takes no notice of her.

The couple from Lancashire, recent arrivals at the guest house, are circling quietly together on the periphery of the bonfire's glow. They are not strangers to Anonyma, having travelled out in the same banana boat. He is a retired stone-deaf building tycoon, a stooping, shambling giant of a man, with freckled skin and wisps of sandy hair; his travelling companion is his secretary, one of those tightly-upholstered middle-aged women whom it is impossible to imagine stripped, or without dentures and rimless spectacles. Each night on the boat they danced and danced to the band. 'Can you 'oom?' he enquired of Anonyma one night. 'Gladys she 'ooms the toon and I can 'ear 'er like a buzzin' in my ear. If you could 'oom we could 'ave a dunce.' Alas, she could not; but they all three had a drink

53

together . . . Now here they are again, still dancing, Gladys from the tensed look about her jaws still humming: a self-sufficient and devoted couple. Not married? No. His wife is in a bin. No matter.

The party begins to disintegrate. Princess has long vanished into the shadows with more than one companion. Unaccustomed to alcohol, Winkliff stands swaying, tranced, one hand upraised in the Boy Scout salute. Presently he keels over and passes out; is scooped up by Louis, whose grandson or maybe great-grandson he is, and stretched out in the nether regions of the hut. Carlotta, surrounded by elderly cronies from the village, has so far preserved a certain dignified distance from the wanton throng; but now, as they thin out she rises, takes her partner and begins to dance The Dance. Carrying her obese frame with buoyant majesty, she slowly rotates, one hand holding out her ample skirts, the other holding aloft a large white handkerchief. Her partner advances, retreats, skips nimbly round and round her in a chassé interspersed with leaps and lunges. He is a toothless, shrivelled ancient, said to be one hundred and ten years old and rumoured to have escaped long long ago from Devil's Island. Now and then she stands stock-still, lowers the handkerchief, allows a ritualistic sexual gesture to ripple through her frame from hips to knees; then starts to rotate in majesty once more. They are dancing a traditional courting dance from Carlotta's native island; and the cronies, knowing better than to join in, participate at a respectful distance by crude gestures and other variants upon the main obliquely indicated theme.

Young Mr de Pas comes crashing down in his Ford, grinds to a halt on the terrace above the bay. He announces himself as usual by four sharp blasts on the horn, two long two short: *Toodle-oo pip pip*! – his signature tune to the initiated. After a brief pause he revs up and crashes off again to some unknown destination: perhaps to pick up

Jackie and drive with her all night, bucketing up hill and down dale as the whim takes him, through pitted by-ways and scarcely beaten jungle tracks. This nocturnal speeding steadies his nerves, according to Miss Stay; Jackie must accept it as her lot: reward or penance who shall say?

Mr Bartholomew, whose steadiness is also so frequently at risk, sustains the rôle of host from first to last. Bottle in hand he scampers here and there, crying: '*Servez-vous, mon vieux*', or ceremoniously murmuring: '*A votre santé.*' His customary equivocal approach has changed to one of eager kindliness; and apart from a first toast to Daisy given in the kitchen – *To my best girl!* – he appears to have cast off the shackles binding him to her. The benefit to him of these liberating occasions lasts for some time. Returned on trial to his own quarters he embarks upon one of his sensible turns and spends quiet evenings reading late by lamplight with the aid of a large magnifying glass. Snatches of poetry continue to escape from him, but at longer intervals and on a subdued, nostalgic note. *Many a green isle needs must be . . . Ah, what avails the sceptred race . . . The wood spurge has a cup of three . . . The old June weather . . . And life's time's fool . . . Over the great Gromboolian plain . . . On the sole Arabian tree . . . So we'll go no more a-roving . . .* Words such as these steal on the visitor's ear.

One day, passing her in the corridor, he stops, takes her hand in his, which is icy, claw-like. He stands in silence, his impenetrably dark spectacles fastened on her face, then murmurs tenderly: 'Tell me your name . . . *Her soft, meandering, Spanish name.*' But another time he stops her to remark quite nastily: '*Daily repenting, never amending*'; followed by an eldritch cackle. Why? What can he mean? Take no notice, take no notice. I am Mrs Cunningham's pet protégée; Miss Stay's little ray of sunshine. What else besides? Victim of Princess's relentless exploitation in the matter of cosmetics (even emery boards and nail scissors have disappeared). What else besides? Playmate of Kit and Trevor . . . She falls upon her bed at intervals, exhausted, lets go of the last shreds of this counterfeit multiple identity; then after a blessed lapse into unconsciousness, slowly, painstakingly starts cobbling it up again, beginning with thoughts of Kit and Trevor.

These are innocuous, even soothing thoughts. Made free, she is now, of their well-appointed bungalow, their books, photographs and records, their experiments in batik work for shirts and scarves; taken in their motor boat for picnics to other idyllic bays, to swim, to collect more shells and coral branches, to watch the pelicans plunge, plunge again for fish, to drink sweet-sour fermenting milk from the green coconuts that Trevor shakes down and opens with his knife, to be photographed by Kit a dozen times. Attractive, creative, sunny-natured pair, with scarcely a grain of malice. Kit's fairly ample means, Trevor's domestic talents, the mixture they share of sophistication and unworldliness combine to make a marriage unshakeably *fidèle* (so they confide) since first they were acquaint. One day perhaps they will go back to England for a good long visit; but here is home now – delicious climate, out of the rat race, busy from morn till night, sufficient unto one another. Family ties, if sparse, are strong. Every other year their widowed mothers, getting on in years but faculties unimpaired and best of friends, come out to spend a happy month or so. Themselves approaching middle age, preserving with care their boyish hips and torsos, they have left youthful ambitions – Kit's to excel as a ballet dancer, Trevor's as a theatrical designer – more or less painlessly behind. They recall the success figures with whom they started out rather as they recall Sibyl Anstey: with nostalgia and regret, but of a special kind: that kind made up of reverence, romance, humility, particular to those whose destiny it is to stoop for and pick up the fallen forever cherished eagle's feather. Oh, Sibyl Anstey, what a personality! – magnetic; what a brilliant conversationalist; above all what a beauty! Something about her larger than life size, a touch of the *monstre sacré* – of for instance Sara Bernhardt – glorious vanishing species. What a dramatic life she must have led, one sensed it . . . No, they had never heard the name Jardine mentioned: always Anstey, Sibyl Anstey – Madame *Anstée* the natives called her. Yes, they had both worked hard on the house of shells, under her supervision. Well yes, they *had* done most of the actual work but it had been such fun and such a privilege; the general design was hers. It was just a rough bathing hut when she arrived. She had it enlarged, made habitable; and then the idea came to her to decorate it, make it a work of art. Basically, of course, it was designed to be her gift to Johnny: she knew that swimming helped him most, both physically and from the point of view of his morale. And then of course he could be alone there, or alone with her. She adored him, no doubt of that. *A great Prince in prison lies*, they heard her once say of him: a quotation, they supposed? And another time she referred to him as her spiritual son. But it didn't quite seem to them like a mother and son relationship. How did Johnny respond? Impossible to tell. He kept one at a distance, dreading pity no doubt, poor sweet. Sometimes they thought he was really a very simple person; sometimes that he was immensely devious, complicated, a smouldering volcano, potentially dangerous. Then, might the volcano become active? Who could say nowadays what might rouse him? He had cultivated unnatural detachment in order to survive. *Think* what he must have looked like in his uniform! – the girls falling like ninepins – the boys as well – I know I would have, says Trevor with an abashed giggle. Difficult to imagine Johnny's real background – home, family, all that, before the war.

He never spoke of it, he had cut himself clean off. They rather thought he had one sister, married, and that his parents were both dead. And Jackie? – what did Jackie make of spiritual sons and mothers? Again, impossible to tell. She'd been much more in evidence when Sibyl first came out – trotting after her, one of her ladies-in-waiting, so to speak. Although presumably it had never been a proper marriage, it had seemed possible, in those first days, before Sibyl Anstey's advent, to consider them in some sense a going concern, an affectionate couple. He was much more helpless then than now; she was energetic, equable, organised his life but didn't fuss him: at least they had never seen him irritated. Had she been in love with him? Probably *not* – at least, one hoped not. Obviously Johnny couldn't be *everybody*'s cup of tea – some girls would have other fish to fry: maybe Jackie was one of these. As time went on, what with Sibyl's take-over and Louis's dedicated service day and night, Jackie lost her job, started to fade out, go her own way. Tony de Pas and that lot much more up her street. Rum taste, but *chacun à son goût*. Johnny didn't object? No one would ever know or guess, much less dare ask what Johnny's feelings were. His reticence was formidable. Perhaps, she suggested, he was rather heartless? – an undeveloped heart? Well, but imagine the adjustments, the disciplines he had been obliged, poor sweet, to practise.

They remembered that Johnny and Maisie had hit it off together. *Maisie?* Yes, Sibyl's granddaughter, who had come out to be with the old lady, had luckily remained until her death. Kit hunts among his myriad prints and negatives: there must be some of Maisie. Any of Sibyl? No, alas! she never permitted him to photograph her: a thousand pities considering the ageless perfection of the bone structure. But here is Maisie.

Incredible! Authentic Maisie, unmistakable. There she stands, very little changed, perhaps even stockier than of yore, planted knee deep in the sea, in a black regulation swim suit, around her neck a lei of various flowers, her rough mane blowing in the breeze. And holding up in her arms, of all things, a plump white naked female infant in a cotton sun bonnet. The wreath is looped around its neck as well as Maisie's, thereby linking them together; and Maisie, all her remembered splendid teeth displayed, is laughing into its face. It is not laughing back. Its spine is stiffened; it wears the maniacal expression of a being helplessly, ferociously at odds with circumstance.

'What about the child?'

Kit looks and laughs. 'Oh yes, poor tot, about to have her swimming lesson.'

'She doesn't look more than eighteen months.'

'About that. Maisie's idea was that if she was dropped in she'd paddle off like a puppy, crowing with delight. *She* didn't see it that way. Crikey, what a little tigress! But she never created when Sibyl was around. She'd roll and splash in the shallows like a water baby. Needless to say that caused ructions.' Some private recollection caused Kit to throw back his head and chuckle. He added: 'How the old lady doted on that child. Her last joy, she said.'

'She adored children. But who is she? Whose child?'

'Maisie's of course.'

'*Maisie's . . .?* It can't be! How extraordinary. She used to say she'd never marry. Whom did she marry?'

But they had never heard mention of a husband. Adopted? That would seem in character. Oh no, it was her own all right. They are fairly sure that Dr Maisie Thomson is an unmarried mother, though none of their business to enquire. Besides, look at the likeness! – not to Mum but Granny. Promise of exceptional beauty.

She seizes the snapshot again and scans it for clues, for likenesses. The bonnet askew over one eye somehow increases the effect of passionate indignation, of imperious

59

will. One fat leg is hooked like a clamp around Maisie's solid waist: not lovingly but in repudiation. In spite of all obscuring factors, there is a suggestion of a familiar cast of countenance.

'What did you say her name is?'

Tanya, they thought, but always called Tarni to rhyme with Barney, and spelt with an 'r' to avoid mispronunciation.

Complex images and sounds arise: Christmas Eve, Mrs Jardine's huge hot kitchen; the voice of Maisie going on and on, conjuring a French river, thick with weeds and water lilies, and someone jumping into them, and someone leaping from the bank to rescue someone tangled in them; and Mrs Jardine advancing with a reverberating remark upon her lips. Gil, a sculptor, killed in action; a shadowy girl he married whose name was Tanya.

'Yes, I see. I remember why Maisie might have called her Tanya.' She goes on staring, amazed. She can all but hear Mrs Jardine remarking at her driest: 'Maisie and her child do not pull well together.' Can it really be that Maisie presented Mrs Jardine with her last joy? – with a true flesh and blood descendant?

'And they were here when she died?'

'Yes, very fortunately.' They rather thought Sibyl had sent for her only living relative. She had grown so frail, almost transparent, but still indomitable in spirit. Maisie was a great support to her. The end was perfectly peaceful: simply, her heart stopped beating one morning in the early hours.

The girls – Carlotta, Princess, Adelina, all of them went far and wide gathering armfuls of lilies, orchids, jasmine, hibiscus, frangipani and wove her a whole sweet-scented coverlet. Next day they made another; last the most magnificent of all. Her face had become smooth, fine, like a carving in ivory. Louis and one of his sons, both men of giant strength, carried her coffin all the way to the cemetery on top of the hill, and the whole village followed, singing hymns and howling, and rigged out in unimaginable Sunday best confections including hats and torturing high heels, to show mourning and respect.

'How she would have enjoyed that! An apotheosis.'

Yes, you could call it that. A unique occasion. Bizarre but moving. No, Johnny didn't go. He took the last blanket of flowers from Maisie, and that evening, with Louis rowing, carried it out to sea and let it float away. Rummaging again through his photographs, Kit picks out one to show her Mrs Jardine's grave. Plain headstone engraved with two words only: SIBYL ANSTEY; no dates, according to her particular instructions. The slab of local stone under which she lies is ringed round with ferns and blossoming shrubs which he and Trevor planted; which they have made it their responsibility to tend. She might like to visit it before she leaves? – and take a photograph to Maisie? Perhaps. She is assailed by a sharp pluck of longing to search out Maisie. Might not something hopeful come from the renewal of that girlhood friendship? Although, imagine admitting to Maisie, that successfully established professional woman, one's own muddles and defeats.

She imagines it. Dr Thomson's consulting room.

'I wonder if you remember me? Rebecca Landon.'

'Can't say I do. Or do I? Yes, good God! – Jess and Rebecca, good little girls put into pinafores for rough games, not allowed to tear their stockings. It all comes back to me.'

'Do you remember one Christmas Eve – when we came to dinner? Jess danced all the evening with – with your brother Malcolm, but we stayed in the kitchen and talked for hours.'

'You don't say! *I* talked, I wouldn't wonder, *you* listened. I wouldn't wonder if your jaw dropped – it often did. Yes, I do remember that evening now you mention it, but we don't dwell on it. They're all dead, every one of them. Jess still alive? Delighted to hear it. Your mother?'

'Oh yes, very much so.'

'Splendid. She was very kind to me. Very *just*. Justice was my passion. What on earth brings you here? What can I do for you?'

'Maisie, I'd like your advice. I'm at a – sort of cross-roads and I wondered . . . I've always wanted to be – well, like you, a doctor.'

'Well, I'm damned. What's bitten you? Aren't you married?'

'No.'

'We'll go into that another time. No children I presume?'

'None.'

'We'll go into *that* another time. Living alone?'

'Not always. Sometimes.'

'A man in your life then. Satisfactory?'

'It was – anyway I thought so. But now it's all over – at least I think so, I'm not sure. I want to change my life.'

'Ever had a job?'

'Several. I've worked in a book shop and a decorating shop – '

'You don't say!'

And I read now and then for a publisher.'

Maisie is silent, a frown drawing her thick brows together. Then she says: 'You're in no state to make decisions, that's for sure. What makes you think you'd make a go of medicine?'

'It interests me so much. I'm not stupid, I'd work hard. I'm not too old, am I?'

'My good girl, let's face it, you're not cut out for it. The training's long and bloody tough, bloody in every sense. You'd never stand it.'

'Psychiatry actually is what I'd like . . . I'd like to specialise in.'

Maisie's silence is magisterial, daunting.

'I know it means years of training – of analysis.'

'And a cracking bore you'd be by the end of it. Sorry to be so blunt, if you do want my advice steer clear of Freud and all those jokers. There are more constructive ways of getting to know yourself.'

'Do *you* know yourself?'

'Yes I do – after a long hard haul. But it's you we're talking about. Why don't you marry whoever it is?'

Out it would all come, the sorry tale, with stammering and attempts at flippancy, and at impartial judgment; and probably final abject sobs. Then Maisie says:

'What induced you to pick such a louse? OK he isn't, but you always were a sucker. Don't blub . . . well, blub away. But blow your nose in a minute or two, there's a love. Chuck it all overboard, it's rubbish anyway, and start again. I'll help if I can, of course I will. I'm very glad to see you. I was very fond of you in the dear dead days – beyond recall, thank God. Remember my grandmother, Sibyl?'

'As if I could forget her.'

'Hmm . . . She made her mark, I will say. Now, are you feeling up to a surprise?'

'A surprise? What sort?'

'In a hundred years you'd never guess.'

Tarni appears – (no surprise) – planted on sturdy legs, exact replica of that old old faded photograph found in a drawer: the child Sibyl in a tartan frock, bows on adorable bare shoulders; angelic face framed in long white-blonde hair, eyes pale, enormous, piercing, full, serious mouth, promising such beauty.

What will Tarni do? Frown? Stiffen herself? Roar? No. After the briefest stare, she runs to me, not Maisie, who says:

'Well, I'm damned! They've clicked'; and proceeds as in former days to tell her story: the story of how Tarni came to be. Says finally: 'You'd better stay for a bit, Rebecca.' A happy time ensues, working in some capacity with Maisie, taken under her wing; the blue-veined child with crystal eyes hovering between them.

The scene cuts off there, brusquely, as always when the images begin to build innocuous self-indulgent fantasies. She dreads to see the face of Anon appear as if through a trap door, watching her with an expression of cold curiosity, as who should say: 'Is she finished off? If not, why not?' Or with that thrust-out lip, flared nostril, crooked smirk of triumph she did glimpse once, for a second. It springs at any moment – perhaps while she is listening to Kit's gramophone records, or watching Trevor's enterprising experiments in batik; or when, as she appears on the Cunningham verandah, Miss Stay calls out with a wave of her clinking glass: 'Here comes our dreamer! Day-dreaming Dinah! Where can her thoughts be?' She comes to a halt, shocked by the frightful notion that Miss Stay is maliciously exercising her paranormal faculties; then advances smiling, shaking her head, as if to suggest the secret romantic nature of her thoughts. Only the wincing man, the Captain looks uncomfortable. His leg twitches, his fierce eye rakes her with what looks like desperation: as if the sight of her threatened him with unacceptable memories of pain. They frighten one another: this will never do. She decides to make a fuss of him. His wife observes this with approval: it is just what he needs, someone well-informed and a good listener; for he is a brainy man and enjoys an exchange of interesting views.

So, by lamplight, with great moths tap-tapping on the shutters, and beneath Joey's watchful presence, he becomes expansive on the subject of military history, flings rum punches helter skelter down his throat, addresses Bobby tenderly, compassionately, produces photographic records of life in Malaya, expatiates on them with a wealth of detail; even, one night, instructs her patiently in the mysteries of bridge. During that lesson his wife put down her sewing and wandered a little way towards the shore. At the turn of the path she was discernible, standing at gaze like Dido, wafting her soul towards the hut. When she returned he threw her sharp teasing words and glances, and she bridled.

Oh, he is a lovable gallant sozzled wreck of an old boy: she would like to hug him. As Miss Stay declares, he is a thorough gentleman, chivalry itself, a heart of gold. He would knock down any cad behaving with conduct unbecoming. Mrs Cunningham's Mummy chose well for her darling daughter.

As the days go on, staring into the dim mirror, as she does obsessively, she begins to see an unfamiliar face: it has become heart-shaped, with cheekbones prominent over attractive hollows, eyes dilated, brilliant. Can she be going into a decline, like a jilted Victorian damsel? She can scarcely eat, she has a constant pain under a lower rib, as if something had got caught up on a hook. If she goes on like this, what with her ethereal pallor, her caved-in stomach, slender limbs, her hair grown long and bleached from letting it float behind her as she swims, she will have become physically unrecognisable. What a shock for him when he appears: for, since he has neither telegraphed nor written, appear he surely must: any day, any moment now. He will alight from a specially chartered biplane . . . No no, of course not, he loathes flying . . . One of the little steamers that ply between the islands will land him one morning or one evening. She will stand still while he walks towards her slowly with a white set face. He will catch his breath and murmur: 'I had to come. I've missed you day and night. Is it really you? You've changed.'

'Yes, I have changed. You have come too late.'

'Too late? You mean you can't forgive me?'

'I mean I don't love you any more.'

Will he believe it? Not he, he's too conceited. A painful scene ensues, at the end of which he slinks away, accepting his dismissal. Next moment back he strides, masterful, passionate, won't take no for an answer, pulls out all the stops.

And then . . . and then? The great scene of reconciliation will not build itself. Alien material keeps intruding. She finds herself conducting a different dialogue; engrossed in a sparkling, caressing, magical exchange of intimacies – *with Johnny*.

Johnny is waxing, the other waning: can it be? In the nick of time he has descended in his car, like an operatic god. She will mount beside him and ascend into the empyrean; will look coldly down upon all once-threatening protagonists.

Her head begins to spin. She seizes the Air Mail block upon which so many letters to Anon have been projected, started, never sent, and scrawls on it wildly the names of these two men, stares at them, obliterates them with fierce strokes, starts again to write, stops, tears off the sheet and crumples it. It must be got rid of. She hurries into her swim suit, flings on her towelling wrap, runs down to the shore, into the sea. When she has swum quite far out, she unclenches her palm, releases the screw of paper it contains, pulls it about until there is nothing left of it but shredded membrane: a taboo object stripped of power.

After that she goes on swimming, floating, sauntering through blue translucent water, imagining herself a specimen of some kind of marine order of creation, propelling itself in a languid, mindless rhythm, cleansed of all remains of human feeling; expecting nothing, no one; not expected anywhere, by anyone. One image continues to tie her to the land: a hut, a sea-grape tree. Round and around it, soaring, dipping, whirling on great white wings, circles the bird laughingly known as Johnny's familiar because of its recurrent mysterious presence and behaviour: as if it carried a message it never managed to deliver. Where is Johnny? No sign of him; but he is there, at the dead centre, hidden, potent.

Why can she not approach him as Ellie does? – Ellie who trips along for a chat and a drink almost as often as the spirit moves her and sits in contemplation, her round eyes vacant, her bow mouth fallen slightly open – a baffled, love-sick innocent. His response is benevolent and humorous, rather like that of a retriever confronted by the blandishments of an ingratiating puppy. Kindness itself, Ellie encourages her new friend to accompany her on these little visits. Perhaps she finds support in another female presence; and such is her increasingly tranced condition when exposed to Johnny, she has ceased to be able to observe, or suspect, Anemone's own intensifying awareness of the beloved object. Indeed, there is almost nothing to observe. Almost nothing. But now and then it is as if an electric current in him started to vibrate; and then his smiles and glances show a heart-stopping intermittent something – challenge? flash of recognition? promise? – tentatively offered, rapidly withdrawn.

Anemone agrees with Ellie: he has simply perfect manners.

As she begins to emerge from the water, the couple of white nurses, Phil and Madge, from Port of Spain, plunge past her brusquely with a grunt for greeting, with flailing arms and violent displacements of the sea around their jaws and shoulders. Phil is a big girl with a face the colour and texture of blancmange. Madge is dark, lean, with sombre eyes and a surly voluptuous mouth. Totally wrapped up in their own affairs, they lie about all day, oiling themselves and one another and murmuring confidentially. Once, passing them, she hears one of them remark on the tail of a yawn: 'Hey ho! I s'pose I'm fickle.' At night they don tight-fitting dance frocks with challenging décolletage and join the crowd at Jackie's on the hill. After one invitation Mrs Cunningham has wiped them off her list. Thoroughly bad taste they are, and man-mad to boot. The Captain neither agrees nor contradicts, but is seen to focus upon their aquatics through his binoculars. Miss Stay's opinion is that they are well-built hard working girls who deserve their holiday; but the words 'mortal treat' do not escape her in connection with their charms; and once or twice their noisy passage through her premises causes her to refer in a general way to the decline of old-world courtesy and gracious manners.

Anonyma has a dreadful dream one night. She is in a hospital ward controlled by Phil and Madge; she has dropped a cup of milk. They flounce past her saying, 'Pick it up yourself, wipe it up yourself, busy in the men's ward, can't attend to you.' She wakes up severely depressed. 'But they really do loathe me,' she says to Ellie later. 'Why do they? They can't think I'm competing.'

'Take no notice, dear,' says Ellie. 'Treat them with contempt. They just naturally hate anyone with breeding, let alone looks. I'd like to see them trying to vamp Johnny, they'd get short shrift.'

In fact they avoid going anywhere near Johnny, doubtless deciding that he is no use, not worth a moment's sexual attention. When Ellie mentions them sarcastically one evening, he raises an eyebrow and says he hasn't noticed them.

Princess hates them with all her heart. 'Dey don'

68

laf plenty,' she says, 'an' deir faces so *wrawng*.' She affects a haughty scowl in imitation before yelling with rude laughter. True it is that they are never seen to laugh, or even to smile. They are cruel harpies, their stone faces symbols of the heartless predatory world.

Young Mr de Pas takes a fancy to organise a day trip in his motor boat by way of celebration of Phil's birthday: a fishing expedition, an evening barbecue in Turtle Bay beyond the Point. Jackie is hostess; indispensable as cooks and fire-makers, Kit and Trevor go along. The Captain needs little pressing to join the party; but his wife develops a touch of migraine and requests that Anemone be spared to keep her company. The two of them spend a peaceful morning washing one another's hair in an egg and brandy shampoo made from a special recipe handed down from Miss Stay's granny, famous in her day for glossy raven locks. 'I can see her now,' says Miss Stay, 'with all that glory flowing down her back at sixty. She could sit on it with ease.' They agree that their rinsed hair has acquired suppleness and sheen, and smells amusingly of brandy. Harold will get a thrill, says Ellie.

Later in the day Miss Stay appears with her Tarot pack, and withdraws with Ellie to the bedroom for her quarterly reading of the cards. When she returns alone, Ellie wears a little frown and hums one of her tunes and seems *distraite*. After a while she remarks that the cards are apt to be what you might call double-faced: you must never leap to conclusions. 'What the future holds is never a certainty, you know, or we wouldn't have free will, which is God's greatest gift to us. Staycie sees *possibilities* – sometimes nice ones, sometimes, well, the opposite. One must keep an open mind. But it's better to be safe than sorry.'

Anonyma ventures: 'Did there seem a not nice possibility?'

After a pause, 'Time will tell,' was the reply. 'Forewarned is forearmed is what I say.'

'One is often warned, inside oneself. As clear as a clear voice speaking. One chooses to ignore it.'

'True,' sighs Ellie. 'Too true.'

Presently she begins in a mock-doleful tremolo: '*The gypsy war-ar-arned me* . . .' cries: 'Oh, that Gracie Fields! Isn't she unique?', smooths away her frown, remarks: 'That's one of the saddest songs in the world, if you come to think of it, yet you double up laughing. What an enigma!'

Miss Stay rejoins them for her evening drink; Ellie suggests a reading for Anemone. But the prophetess reacts evasively, saying: 'Not yet, dearie, better wait a while'; then sensing consternation, plunges into verse: '*Birdie wait a little longer, till the little wings are stronger.*'

'Staycie doesn't mean you're not quite – anything of a mental nature, do you, Staycie?' Ellie is severe, reproachful.

'Indeed not, no indeed! She's our ray of sunshine.'

'Weak. I know I am,' quavers the culprit.

'No no. Still just a wee thought easily upset – and who can wonder? But getting steadier. More light in your aura, lovely peacock blue returning. Every day that passes steadier and steadier. It's a joy to behold.'

'Staycie sets great store on steadiness, don't you, Staycie?'

'Ah, it has stood me in good stead.' Clapping hand to mouth, she flings her legs up with a stifled hoot. 'The Lord be praised for the Captain's absence! Yes, girls, I learnt soul-steadiness the hard way. I went down into the depths to dredge for it.'

Yes, it is Miss Stay's equipment for dealing with life's frets and shocks. She went through fire, tempest, earthquake, heaven knows what to gain it; and now she is as mad as a March Hare and as steady as a rock. Prop and stay (ha! ha!) to many a weaker vessel, star to wandering barks, unshaken both in tolerance and loving kindness. Can it be that she is some species of angelic being in disguise; and although her racked body has accepted the travesty, it twitches and jerks with yearning to throw it off and reveal her radiant, golden-winged, as in old fairy tales and legends?

With a swift unaccountable lift of her spirits, Anonyma says, under her breath: 'Anything might happen.'

'What was that?. asks Ellie.

She shakes her head, laughs. Miss Stay nods in strong approval of the laugh.

And what did happen?

The day ended with a gift to Anonyma, the first, from Johnny. Without warning, Johnny turned, as if – as if acknowledging, or surrendering, and possibly with a touch of irony beneath the look he bent on her: Johnny turned suddenly and gave her the taste of joy. Pure, piercing, unmistakable, astounding taste of joy.

What happened? A late swim from Johnny's boat by starlight and the light of Louis's lantern, leaving Ellie to prepare supper in the hut. He swam far out, away from where she circled quietly just beyond the lantern's soft corona. Then back he came, she watched him, thrusting through the water with powerful strokes, his great shoulders looming as he came abreast of her and passed her without a word or glance. Then suddenly he turned, swam back, swept her into his arms, gave her a kiss. Not smiling. Saying nothing. A cold, salt kiss. Cheek pressed to cheek they remained; then broke apart. The boat came gliding up on silent oars, she swam away to shore, crossed the white sands, dressed again as usual behind the hut, joined Ellie who, mixing avocado salad, exclaimed with dismay at sight of her wet hair so recently fortified with egg and brandy.

They came out and sat on the steps, under the light of the two hanging lamps. Presently Ellie murmured: 'Look!' with a sharp intake of breath. Johnny was walking towards them, slowly, his arm round Louis's shoulder, Louis's arm around his waist: walking upright, firmly. He had changed in the boat, and wore a blue shirt open at the neck, white linen trousers. 'You see, he can,' breathed Ellie. 'I knew he could. Oh, doesn't he look gorgeous?' Then, as they came nearer: 'Better not seem to be watching them perhaps'; and she got up and slipped away into the kitchen. But, as if it were an everyday occurrence, or as if it were all happening in a dream, Anonyma ran forward to join them where they now stood waiting, smiling. They loomed impressively above her, matched in height, with a parallel display of strong white teeth; and from the shafts of light cast by the house lamps their eyes reflected an equal glitter. They moved into the shadow of the sea-grape tree, where without a word Louis left him propped against the trunk and vanished into the house.

'Louis seems to trust you,' said Johnny. 'It's a great compliment.'

'Yes, you're quite safe with me.'

'Am I? Well . . .' He laughed.

'You won't fall.'

'No. Still, you'd better keep close.'

She came close, and they clasped one another.

'You looked so extraordinary, you and Louis.'

'How, extraordinary?'

'Like brothers somehow. Not brothers of today. From another age.'

He laughed again. 'Sort of twin monsters? Perhaps we are. Are *you* safe, do you suppose?'

They kissed again. Pressed to his chest she noticed for the first time that he wore a locket or medallion on a long gold chain. Presently she said: 'Johnny, to see you

walking! I didn't know – at least I wasn't sure. I think I
did know.'

'Once in every hundred years,' he said. 'Like the aloe.'

'I do love you, Johnny.'

He did not reply, but covered her face with light kisses;
then said: 'Come. We won't tempt Providence'; and
walked without faltering towards his dwelling. Louis
darted out noiselessly with a cane armchair into which he
tumbled, saying: 'A drink, Louis. And one for the lady';
and after they were brought and they were alone again:
'Not a graceful performance. Still, it may improve.
You're wondering – if I can, why don't I more?'

'Too tiring?' she suggested.

'Not really. Well, a bit perhaps. I'm not taking any
chances.'

'Is it a secret?'

'For the present.'

'Who knows? – besides Louis and – now, me?'

'Ellie, presumably. But you may have noticed, she
prefers to ignore such goings-on.'

'Not that exactly. She doesn't quite dare to make it
real – I suppose because she cares so much. Or perhaps
she's afraid that if it's true, you might get up and go.
What about Miss Stay?'

'Oh, Staycie gave me the first shove. So she believes at
least. I dare say she did.'

'I thought it was Mrs Jardine – Sibyl . . .'

'Oh yes,' he said after a pause, evasively. 'She worked
on me, of course. In her own way.' He laughed again,
abruptly.

'Your wife knows?'

'Not my wife.' His smile broadened, this time not a
pleasant smile. He felt for, and lit a cigarette, then
continued slowly: 'One day I shall walk up that hill and
enter my own house. It may take time. But I'll get there.'

She looked at him, startled by his expression, unable to

interpret it. A slight distortion seemed to have occurred, making him look almost ugly. Then his odd wing-like eyelids lifted, he looked at her sharply out of his cold clear eyes and burst out laughing. 'Don't look like that,' he said. 'Damn it, it is my house. I planned it, paid for it. I'm Scotch, you know, I'm close, I like value for my money. My desirable residence has gone down in the world. It stinks of riff raff, parasites, squatters, and their bloody boringness. I'll kick them out one day. I aim to, anyway.'

'I haven't seen your house, except in the distance,' she said cautiously.

'No, and you won't either. I wouldn't let you touch it with a barge pole. Pity. It's a pleasant house – or was. I'd like to show it to you. I'd like you to stay there.' She flushed with gratified surprise. 'I've got the instincts of an average householder, you know.' He threw an ambiguous glance over his shoulder, up and down the shell-encrusted walls. 'Do you think this rococo bijou setting really suits me?'

'I suppose – not really.'

'Not really quite *me*.' He affected a nasal pansy drawl. Then, after a pause during which he seemed pleased to have made her laugh, he added soberly: 'Not but what I'm grateful for it, very, very grateful. It's been a godsend. Somewhere to be private; and space all round me. But I can't help wondering sometimes, what's the point.'

'Won't you ever come back to England?'

'Of course I want to go back. Long to. But not unless I'm – completely independent. Which as you see I'm not.'

'You will be, Johnny.'

He shrugged; then burst out with furious impatience: '*Every day and in every way I get better and better*. Actually, I think I'm stuck for life . . . Why do you look at me like that?'

'You make my heart ache.'

'Poor you. How uncomfortable. That's one thing I'm

spared. No heart, no heartaches. See what an unpleasant character I am.'

'I like unpleasant characters.'

'I believe you do, I'm afraid you do. Something tells me that's your trouble.'

The silence that ensued was intimate and full of tension. He broke it to say quietly: 'No. Judging from what my antennae tell me, let alone the papers, let alone our wise splendid far-seeing politicians, the world is going blind and deaf. *Millions* of people will be homesick soon, you'll see. If one can't alter a single damn thing, one might as well stay put.' He looked out to sea, she watched his profile. 'Besides, I don't fancy leaving Louis. I'm attached to him.'

'It would break his heart.'

'Yes. Louis has got a heart.'

Louis appeared, carrying tall glasses brimming with amber liquid, fruit, ice, slivers of aromatic herbs and Ellie joined them, whom Johnny teased, joked with as usual. The rage, or whatever had been the pressure choking him subsided so quickly and completely it seemed that she must have dreamed that she had felt its crushing impact.

But the beautiful buoyant strangeness continued to prevail; as if they had been lifted, for an hour or so, into a dimension of less density; as if Time had thrown a loop around them, leaving them islanded, free of its main troubled and obstructed coil.

Once, getting up to take a cigarette from him, she stooped to blow the match out and put her lips to his hair. He stretched a hand out and held hers for a moment. Ellie did not notice.

'Such a happy evening,' said Ellie when finally, after midnight, they wished him goodnight and went their separate ways. 'A happy happy evening.'

*

But, for Anonyma, the night has only just begun. Stretched on her bed, two candles in glass funnels burning on the bedside table, thinking of Johnny, still savouring, with amazement, the taste of joy, she sees another figure rise: Mrs Jardine is present. She has come back, moves close, seems to be watching intently just the other side of the mosquito net. White face, pale blazing sapphire eyes; wrapped in a blue cloak. Mrs Jardine's once-favoured child starts to spin this way, that way, backwards through a Hall of Mirrors, chasing elusive identities. How crowded, empty, how far away, how near the time seems between now and the primrose-picking candidate's first step into the world of myth and magic.

'Mrs Jardine!'

The figure wavers and dissolves; the voice replies: 'You called me.'

'Did I? No. Yes, perhaps. Is it really you again?'

'Who else?'

'You remember me?'

'Faintly. The picture kindles only faintly – when you call me by that name. It is not my name.'

'Mrs Jardine is not your name?'

'No. It has been discarded.'

'Sibyl?'

'Sibyl will do well, *Your* name? I am not sure of it.'

'I am Rebecca.'

'Ah, Rebecca, yes. A curious child. Simpleton. Reckless.'

'Reckless, was I? To myself I was always the reverse. Timid. Often frightened.'

'*Cela n'empêche pas* . . . Easily impressed, imposed upon.
Oh, I saw trouble ahead for you, a troubled destiny.'

'Like yours.'

Silence. Then: 'Possibly a likeness in our natures, yes. I may have recognised it. Extravagant expectations.

Well – they must be paid for. I paid.'

'Truth was your ruling passion, so you used to say.'

'I said that, did I? Yes. Do you care for truth?'

'Yes, passionately.'

'But how carefully we choose our truths, how cunningly we select.'

'Your words sound mocking, harsh. You spoke differently to me once: as if you burned with passionate conviction. Oh, I lived in your shadow for a while! – or should I say your light? I thought myself your chosen one, your confidante. I was your slave, your messenger.'

Long pause. 'Well well . . . Matters of no importance.' But the voice was shaken, had lost its note of sharp authority.

'You said once, of paramount importance. Have you forgotten? Do you prefer not to remember?'

Another long pause. 'I dreamed many dreams, Rebecca. You played your part in them.' Now the voice became nostalgic, tender. 'We conspired to dream, my love. Such perilous stuff must be stripped off when we discard our bodies.'

'Then death is oblivion. Sleep and forgetting.'

'Nonsense, child. With whom are you conversing?'

'Mrs – The ghost of Mrs Jardine, I suppose.'

'You must learn to be more accurate. Long ago I told you so. Why do you laugh?'

'Because it's really you! – you haven't changed. You were always so didactic – always instructing me.'

'You had aptitude.'

'Now you sound mocking, cold again. Were you all the time deceiving me?'

'How, deceiving you?'

'About love for instance. And caring nothing for the world's opinion. All the things you went on and on about. I swallowed every word.'

Another silence; then the voice said softly: 'Well, love

77

is all. I did not deceive you, little Rebecca – Mrs Jardine did not deceive you. But in some ways she has grown rather shadowy. Old unhappy far-off things, you know. Bitter bitter lessons – learnt and not learnt. Let us not dwell too much on her. She was not wholly admirable.'

'I adored her.'

'You were a dear child. I begin to see you clearly now. Rebecca – Laura's grandchild. A touch of Laura in her.'

'You said so. That's why you – why I thought you loved me. It was because of her that we were allowed to know you. Oh, I remember everything! The blue door in the wall – it opened – we stepped in! Such narrow bread and butter lives we led outside. Inside was magic – honeydew.'

The voice started to murmur, as if in sleep or trance. 'Children running in the garden, playing, laughing – just as I had dreamed. Oh! I am there again. I see them. Darlings. *Beautiful*. I thought . . . no matter. A cloud comes over. Sorrow, sorrow.' The voice broke, sobbed, faded out; picked up again to say: 'But Laura, who was your grandmother: indeed I loved her – love her. We have been together in one relationship or another through many lives on earth. I woke up after death to see her beside me, smiling, welcoming me. But she has gone a long way on. She visits me from time to time: sheds light on me, and love.'

'Please ask her to shed light on me.'

'I will. The beauty of spiritual forms like hers is unimaginable. You would not see them – too bright for you.'

'But not for you, I suppose.'

Appreciative chuckle. 'Now you are mocking me. Well . . . sometimes my eyes open, I have glimpses. But when she met me – when I first arrived – she came in her old guise – in a crinoline dress that I particularly loved. To reassure me.'

'There was a man you loved, called Paul.'

'Yes, yes – Paul. But he is not for you.'

'Of course not! He died long ago – before I was born. You can't still be so possessive? – jealous of the dead?'

'Jealous? – no indeed. The dead? I see I must go slowly with you, you are very backward, stupid. I meant, beware of such as he. The lordly, the destroyers.'

'That sounds like the old you – like Mrs Jardine, since you make some sort of distinction, incomprehensible to me, between Mrs Jardine and – '

'Sibyl. Ah well, it is confusing; and as I say you are rather dull. However I must admit I am still confused myself. I only know that Sibyl is my true name. It is Sibyl that dear Laura knows; and Paul.'

'You are with him, then?'

'We have been re-united. There was much to disentangle, to undo. Torments of self-imprisonment to break out from. But nothing is lost, Rebecca, nothing of love is lost.'

'Then Harry too is with you?'

Another pause. 'Dear Harry. We have met of course. But no, we are not together. Harry has gone to his own place. As we all do.'

'I remember him. And Cherry.'

'Ah, Cherry, my little one – what joy! Incredulous joy! Laughter! Tears of joy! Laughter and tears together. Her hand in his once more. Miraculous journeys – into earth's very heart. Into the scintillating dark of ocean beds, into strange countries of the air. Nourished by divine sonorities, by essences of light and colour. Oh, ineffable experiences!'

'Yours as well?'

'No, not mine. I am still too – There is nothing of Ariel in me. But I have news of them, my delicate spirits, never at home in your dense sphere. *One* slipped away betimes; the other was condemned to stay behind. A ghost man, drained. His light feet in the world left not a trace, not even of the blood they bled. I catch your scurrying rejecting thoughts. How, by whom condemned, you ask? Maybe an old debt he may have stayed to pay – *chosen* to pay. His silence went on sheltering me: a shroud of unaccusing silence into which, when his heart broke – I broke it – I went on creeping, *to listen to the shot*.'

'What do you mean? What shot?'

'A casual shot – one sunny afternoon. Experiment, infatuation, animal urge . . . call it what you will. I shot love out of the sky. Down, down it fell; one thud, like a dead bird. Finished.'

'You mean . . . you mean you were unfaithful?'

'That is what I mean.'

'Paul?'

'No, nonsense, rubbish, nothing of that nature. That was incorruptible – we made it so in spite of – all. No, no. Just a passer-by. I beckoned – or he beckoned – what matter which of us? *Hi! handsome hunting man!* It was like that.'

'Harry could not forgive you?'

'Harry – *a dû constater* what he could never have imagined: that I could be base. It was a shock. It killed our marriage. He worshipped me, you see. Worship comes before a fall. However, after the – discovery, he continued to protect me. A perfect gentleman, was Harry.'

'So you always told me.' *The recollected flick in the pupils of the eyes, the drumming fingers, the histrionic turn of speech . . .*

'We were a chaste couple for the remainder of our marriage.' Then the voice rose, passionately assertive. 'But Harry was not destroyed, no matter what they whispered – the evil tongues, I was not deaf to them, the sneering lips, I was not blind! His spirit remained intact – that was my consolation.'

'Did he stop loving you?'

An entirely unfamiliar voice, after a pause, said quietly, reflectively: 'I think he did not stop. Love dies hard, you know. But he did not like me any more, my dear. That hurts one's self-esteem. However this is an old story. We have forgiven one another, gone our ways.'

'One another?'

'Yes.'

'Why should the one betrayed need to be forgiven?'

Sound as of someone laughing – a harsh sound. 'I recall a child with somewhat simplistic moral views. I sometimes marvelled. Oh, I was aware of being strong meat for such as she. But innocents, I told myself, are equipped with phenomenal digestions.'

'So you did have qualms?'

Another laugh. 'No, I did not. The woman you remember did not deal in qualms.' Then briskly: 'Well now! – these questions of treachery, forgiveness, are troubling you at present?'

'Torturing me. Help me, take pity on me.'

'I do pity you, poor child. I doubt if I can help you.'

'What am I to do? How can I live like this, in exile, in suspense? Am I unlovable? If so, how can I bear to live? I cannot bear it.'

'That is yesterday talk. Tonight life is more than bearable again. Is it not so? Be truthful!'

'Can it be so? Yes, it is so. But what has happened? What is going to happen?'

'That I cannot tell.'

'And why have you come back?' No answer. 'Now and then, since I've been here, I have almost seen you.'

'Indeed! What makes you think so?'

'You know why . . . In that blue cloak of yours.'

'Oh, my blue cloak. It covers him.'

'And you are on the watch – as once you were before, so I was told. Watching me, I suppose.'

Silence. Then: 'He cannot help you. Don't imagine it.

Do not presume on his – response.'

'As if I would!'

'Well, we shall see.'

'And he has already helped me. The voice in my ear that went on whispering: "*End your life*" has ceased.'

'I am aware of that. How you would rue it, should you have succeeded. Nothing – less than nothing – solved, all to do again. A grotesque mistake. I have told him so, more often than he knows. You had good instincts once, Rebecca: surely they told you that life goes on – relentlessly one might say. I hear your thoughts – arrogant, summoning your sceptical defences, your intellectual nihilism – '

'No, not that.'

'Stupidity, then, if you prefer. Once you had imagination: you have let it atrophy. Wake up, Rebecca! Yes, I am naming you. *Wake up, Rebecca!*'

'Yes, I must wake up. This is another dream: but not a bad dream. Where can it be coming from? Some of my dreams burn me, soil, claw at me – monsters from the pit. This is quite different. I'm still not sure though if you wish me well. Why am I not afraid of you? Long ago I had a dream of you that terrified me. Now you have lost your power. I feel – forgive me – I seem to feel sorry for you. Are you – forgive the question if it is tactless, naïve – are you an Unquiet Spirit?'

Silence. A chuckle. Silence. 'Not exactly. But love, concern, still draws us back to earth. Thoughts directed to us, strong thoughts, urgent, seek us out, call us, touch us: we are connected, we respond. That is the law of love.'

'Of hate as well?'

'We will not speak of hate.'

'Shall we speak of Ianthe?'

'My daughter. No, we will not speak of her.'

'Poor Sibyl. Does he call to you? You know who I

mean.'

A pause. A sigh. No answer.

'Can you help him?'

After a pause, a broken mutter, the words 'my punishment . . .' otherwise impossible to catch.

'He doesn't want your help?'

'He does not wish to be saved.'

'What do you mean?'

'We shall see.' Something nameless, like a groping tentacle, reached out. '*Pray*, Rebecca. We must pray.'

'I don't pray. Do *you* pray? That seems strange.'

'I am learning.' A humble voice.

'Talking to God! I can't imagine it. I don't want to learn.'

'What is it that you do want, Rebecca? Ah, I know! No need to pretend, protest. You want a lover.'

'Not *any* lover. I'm not like you – promiscuous.'

'To be back in the time of roses, that is what you want. To loose your hair and be undressed and bathed and scented: prepared for – ah! what wild expectations and fulfilments! Not only that, you say, not erotic pleasure only. No, of course not! Let us not be coarse, explicit. I too preferred reticence, hated immodesty, rejected the crude thick words. Of course that is only part of what you long for. You yearn to be telling yourself: "I am precious, preferred above all other women . . ." scarcely daring to believe it; but then how smoothly, rapidly accepting it! You thought you had known love before, *he* thought so too. But past experience was schoolroom stuff! This is the true, the once-in-a-lifetime love. Each of you the other's bright particular star, fixed in the firmament. Ah, and how effortless from your galactic heights to condescend to those less fortunate! – to show gracious gratitude for services formerly taken for granted; to listen patiently to bores, be considerate to parents and other impedimenta usually neglected. Impregnable within your luminous cocoon, you fly in sure and certain expectation to answer the distinguishable bells: the telephone voice that does not need to name itself; the post that brings the letter whose very envelope causes your heart to constrict with the mystery of the recognised handwriting.'

'The letter, yes! Where is it? When will it come? What will it say? Has it been lost? intercepted? wrongly addressed? Do I wait here for it, in this mad limbo? How shall I dare to open it? Shall I tear it up unread? Must I return without it? Will all be as before? Shall I telegraph *Returning Meet me*, and find him waiting, with the same face – or with a changed face, sheepish? pompous? wary? hostile? *A stranger with a murderer's face?*'

'Hush! Calm yourself. I am no fortune teller, I cannot read your future. Besides, this man is not important.'

'There now, as usual you contradict yourself. You are wicked, heartless, my father always said so. You tell me love is all – and then you shrug your shoulders. Love is consuming me, I tell you. I am sick, I must die.'

'Nonsense, you will not die. *Men have died and worms have eaten them* . . . you know the rest.'

'Well then, I shall do as I was told. I will trust my unhappiness and great good will come to me. Great good will come to me! I have decided: I will make those words my daily bread. Whatever he says, *whatever* he does, whatever, I will go on trusting him. I will trust the promises he made me, and I will trust his broken promises, his treacheries. So I cannot lose, I am bound to win, I am bound to . . .?'

Silence. Silence. Then a brisk counselling voice: 'Your mother now, Rebecca, such a charming woman. Upright, unselfish, unworldly, loyalty itself. Strong moral principles yet tolerant. Such a help long ago with that difficult girl Maisie. Full of years now, but all her faculties. Creep back home and take a rest. Surround yourself with innocence and comforts. Hot milk, soft single chintzy bed, regular meals, family news and photographs. What a treat for her, what pleasure it would give her.'

'No, it would not. The mere sight of me would utterly dismay her. Trouble, trouble, she would guess. Were I to break down and tell her, she would give dreadful good advice. Strange but true, families are the cruellest company in these predicaments: forcing you back to the roots, and oh! how the roots tug, threaten, ache; whispering the old competitive comparisons, guilts, atavisms, insecurities. Plain, pretty; clever, stupid; naughty, good; bad marks, top marks; spiteful; selfish; jealous; unfair; unkind; unjust; your fault; my fault; his fault; her fault; best loved, not loved, lonely, lonely, failure FAILURE . . .'

'Well well! – what a macabre picture – hysterical, ridiculous. I had no family to cushion me – a bitter deprivation. I tried but failed to found one – my own flesh and blood to hand my treasures down to. *Wait though! – one* has arrived on earth, a true descendant, just as I prepared to leave. Made in my likeness – '

'Tarni?'

'Bearing the fatal gift of beauty. I shall watch over her. But to revert: your father now, he thought me wicked, did he? He thought me something else as well, I fancy, in his salad days. Young men are not averse to wicked women. Our paths crossed once upon a time – oh yes! They crossed. But what a family man he did become in later years: so protective of his lambs.'

'He is dead, I suppose you know.'

The sense of someone smiling, an ambiguous smile.

'Yes. Our paths crossed once again, but briefly. I am no longer anathema to him. Humour saved us – humour, compassion, repentance – ' The voice took on a note of passion. 'Ah, the good old days! Horsewhipping and high melodrama! Fallen women, ruined, disgraced for ever, better dead. Oh, those were stirring, titillating times!

Infamous humbug, abominable cruelty in every walk of life. How we were spat upon, humiliated, we women with the courage to defy convention and win our independence. *We* fought to win *your* freedom. Don't forget it.'

'I won't forget it. But must you be still so strident on that topic?'

'What topic?'

'Emancipation of women – all that stuff. You were such a bore.'

A tremor, as of one shocked – or hurt perhaps. The voice said uncertainly: 'The young are . . . Was I tedious, strident? These realms I inhabit now are fluid: one is apt to reassume discarded garments. Earth memories flood in, the old bitternesses. Where I am now, those you refer to so contemptuously free themselves from those particular chains that were so lacerating. Chains of emancipation. But the suffering, the dedication, the sisterliness in selfless striving – these are not made naught. They form – how shall I say? – a spiritual essence which enfolds them, in which they can bathe and heal them of their grievous wounds. You are far from their eminence, Rebecca.'

'Oh, I'm sure! I am worthless, self-indulgent, self-involved, far from *your* eminence as well. Completely, totally non-eminent.'

Silence again, a puzzled silence. Then doubtfully:

'I am too didactic?'

'Well – you do go on, you always did. I wondered what would happen if I teased you. Did anybody, ever?' The air was beginning to become charged, electric. 'It's better to be teased than worshipped, isn't it?' Pressure, agitation grew. 'Did anybody love you enough for that?'

'Yes, oh yes! And laughter! – laughing together. Our souls laughed together.'

'You miss that?'

The voice sank; sweat broke out on her to hear it

say triumphantly:

'Though my cloak covers him I have not altogether shed it. There's a riddle for you! *My old dexterity in witchery gone:* I read that once, I liked it. Not gone, my old dexterity, no, not gone! My beauty back! I lived for beauty – what I sowed I reap. All beautiful, my lovers! – the last the most beautiful of all. I see him as you cannot, I see him in his whole and perfect body. We are well matched for beauty. He is mine. Mine!'

'*You are wicked, Mrs Jardine, wicked!*'

Springing up in bed she gasps aloud these words; and whatever it was – hallucination, spirit visitor, thins away on a thread of mocking laughter. She flings aside the mosquito net, runs to the window, pushes the shutters open, leans out. Dark: no sign of dawn. Throughout immensities of lustred indigo the great stars blaze, pulsate, swing towards earth as if to listen to her multitudinous vibrations. Frogs. Cicadas. Dogs far and near. Moths. Fireflies in cloudy scintillating swarms.

In her shack Daisy stamps once, twice. Can she be missing her mad master? He is absent for the night, gone, according to Miss Stay, to visit an old friend, the Roman Catholic priest on the other side of the island. It seems unlikely, yet the guest-house car certainly removed him, spruced up beyond recognition by Miss Stay, around teatime. Mercifully, Phil and Madge are also absent: living it up with young Mr de Pas and Jackie and the rest, heaven knows where. Miss Stay has elected to sleep down there in the bungalow with Ellie in case the Captain should turn up late – or not at all. From the direction of the Lancashire couple's suite issues the reassuring sound of snoring.

Nothing unusual or threatening. Two more days and then I shall be leaving, accompanied by Kit and Trevor, in a spanking new fast German pleasure cruiser from Port of Spain. One of the Mums has had a stroke, both lads must hurry to her bedside. What a piece of luck! No matter what's in store I shall be cherished for ten days, played with, lots of jokes and drink.

And never see Johnny again.

The wind of night stirs suddenly, breathes out a perfumed breath that dies away with a sound like a long sigh.

Something surprising happens. Far down in the huge well of stars and darkness, where the hut, the sea-grape tree must be, as if a lid had opened to show a lambent eye, a light appears, stares back at her unwinkingly. Johnny has lit his lamp.

Is calling?

The door was open; she went in and found him lying on his bed, reading, still dressed as when she had last seen him.

He said quietly: 'Anonyma.'

'Were you expecting me?'

'What have you got in your hair? Come here. Sit down.' He took her hand and pulled her down to sit near the head of the bed. 'Fireflies! Two – three. How pretty.' He brushed them off and they fell on the floor, extinguished.

'Do you mind my coming, uninvited, at this compromising hour?'

'Not in the very least.'

His manner was the usual one of formal courtesy. What to do, say, next?

'No mosquito net?'

'Not necessary. Mosquitoes seem to be repelled by me. Or the duppies frighten them.'

'I wish I repelled them. But they're not the worst. There's some horrible invisible something in the sand. I was stupid enough to go barefoot the first few days, and oh! my feet. They still itch.'

'Your poor feet, what a shame! I'm afraid you're a

temptation to the local carnivores.' He took up her hand again, turned it over, as if examining it carefully, put it down. 'Hands all right? Very pretty hands.'

She said shyly: 'Thank you.' Then, after a pause: 'Were you expecting me?'

He shut his book with a marker in it, looked at her quickly, looked away. 'Well – it's nice,' he said, as if making a difficult admission. 'I rather wanted to come to *you*. But I couldn't. So – '

'Have you been asleep?'

'No. Have you?'

'Not really. I was looking out of the window and I saw your light. I'd been thinking about you. So I thought I'd come.' Vivid colour rose suddenly in his face; and she thought with surprise: Can he be blushing? Addressing his averted cheek, she continued less nervously: 'Besides, I'd been having such an extraordinary – sort of dream. I had to come.'

'Why not?' He sat up and looked round his austerely furnished cell. 'Not many amenities, I fear. Would you like an armchair? A drink?'

'No, thank you. Where is Louis?'

'Gone fishing. Did your dream frighten you?'

'Not till the last bit of it. But then yes, very much. This is a place where queer things happen, isn't it?' He glanced at her. 'As if,' she went on lamely, 'one was between two worlds, or on the fringe of another and could step over very easily. One does step over.' It was a query but he did not answer, and she finished: 'I wasn't asleep, yet I wasn't awake. I was having – I thought I was having – a long talk with someone.'

'Oh, really?' He raised an eyebrow. 'It sounds confusing.'

'With Mrs – with Sibyl.'

'How unnerving.' His face and his voice were impenetrable.

'Johnny, do you have dreams?'

'About her? No, never. Not about her or anyone. I never dream. It doesn't do.'

'How can you prevent it? No one can.'

'Oh yes one can.'

'How?'

'By staying awake.'

'Is that what you do? You don't sleep?'

'Not much. Off and on. Cat naps. Quite enough. I read quite a bit.' He picked up the book he had laid down and said with a faint smile: 'The History of Henry Esmond. Very enjoyable. I wasn't born a reader. Sibyl started my education – from scratch, I must admit. Most of these books are hers.' He indicated well-filled bookshelves along one wall.

'She left them to you?'

'Yes, she did.'

His voice remained dismissive; but she took the plunge.

'You never seem to want to talk about her.'

'Not really. Not . . . what's the point?' He sounded awkward, embarrassed.

'What's the point because she is dead, you mean?'

'Partly I mean that.' Heaving a sigh, he flung an arm across his eyes, for all the world like a sulky boy, cross-questioned.

'Are you cross?'

'No. But talking . . . All this *talk*, it's so tedious. It never stops.'

'I'm sorry, darling.' She stooped and kissed his cheek; seeming to see in a flash what underlay his formality, his winning social smile, his attentiveness and joking ways. They were a fortress he had raised around his ruined life. If his defences came down he could only stammer. Presently he said:

'No need to sound so contrite. Don't imagine the subject of Sibyl is too sacred – or too painful. I miss her, of course.

90

She was extremely good to me. But – it's a long long story. Boring. I hate post mortems. The point is, must we talk about her *now*?'

'Of course not. Then we won't.'

'Another time, perhaps. There's plenty of time . . . Or isn't there?'

'You mean, how much longer shall I be here?'

'I suppose that's what I mean.'

'Two more nights; and then I cross to Port of Spain with Kit and Trevor, to catch a boat.'

'For England. What an enviable prospect.' He had dropped his arm, but his eyes remained shut. 'I can't *think* what you're doing here. Why you ever came.'

'I could tell you – try to. But it would be another long long story, which you would certainly find boring. It doesn't make much sense, even to me.'

'I realised,' he said politely, 'that you'd had some sort of a knock.'

'I expect Ellie told you.'

'She didn't actually – not in so many words.'

'You mean, she hums *There's a silver lining* when my name crops up.'

He grinned and nodded.

'I'll tell you briefly,' she said, 'and get it over. I came, I mean I thought I was coming with a person who – wanted to go far away from England. He asked me to come with him: in fact, that was the crux of the whole idea, that we should go away together. It sounded like Paradise, this island. He'd heard of it.'

She stopped. The great confession sounded lame and feeble.

'I see,' said Johnny. 'Perhaps he'd heard of the orchid, the one found only here. Is he interested in orchids? I can't seem to get a picture of the chap.'

'Nor can I. Not any more. No, he's not interested in orchids. He wanted to write – he's a writer – about the

Caribs. And he wanted to burn his boats. But he must have changed his mind.'

'But you didn't?' He sounded perplexed, impatient.

'Why did I come alone, you mean. I didn't know he'd changed his mind till I was on the boat. The telegram was waiting for me in my cabin. I couldn't think what to do. I couldn't get off the boat, it was too late, and anyway nowhere to go back to. I hid in my cabin, pretending to be seasick. After three days I sent him a cable. I can't remember what I said, quite. I thought he would follow by the next boat, or get on a plane or something. "Thought" is the wrong word. I was beginning to get frightened: the walls of my cabin were starting to close in and suffocate me. So I went up on deck. But that was worse. I didn't know any longer who I was. I sweated with panic; but nobody seemed to notice anything odd. There were attempts to get me to join in fun and games. There was a Colonel who wanted to marry me, would you believe it! I told him: "I'm not what you think I am," meaning I was a walking dummy, automatic. But he thought I meant I was a tart and said he'd overlook it. He must have been mad too.'

Johnny opened his eyes, shot her a searching glance, smiled faintly.

'Yes,' she said, 'I know it's funny. Well, that's all. Here I am. I haven't heard a word. I'm going back. What will happen then I've no idea.'

'You've got a home or something, I suppose?'

'My mother still lives in our old home, where I was born. An aunt of mine, a widowed sister, lives with her. They worry because I don't get married. The reason I don't is this man. But I don't want to say any more, you don't want to hear any more about him, do you?'

'Not really.'

She watched him for a few moments, noting the curious slanting cut of his long eyelids, their trick of lifting and dropping lazily, like a pair of black-fringed wings. She said:

'I'll just finish relating my history. When my father died he left us each some money. One of my sisters and I clubbed together to buy a small cottage – it's in Berkshire, on the downs. But that sister did get married so now it's mine. Sometimes I share it with a girl friend who likes gardening, or I'm alone, or with the person we don't want to talk about. He's got a flat in London, and that's where I often am – or have been. Do you think it's all over? I do.'

He remained silent, his eyelids lowered still; then said, without expression: 'The girls I knew – one or two – had some sort of a job. But that was in the war, of course.'

'I've had several jobs.' She felt stung, as if he had reproached her. 'I quite agree, it's time I changed my life. It's an idiotic waste, keeping oneself free, or half free anyway, in case – It serves me right, it's – '

'Don't cry!' He caught her hand again, kissed it. 'You're cold, you're shivering. Are you cold?'

'Yes.'

'Come here, lie down, get warm.'

She lay down by his side and went on shivering violently. He dried her tears with his pocket handkerchief, pulled a soft grey and brown striped rug from the foot of the bed, covered them both, put his arms tightly round her, saying: 'If you don't mind rather a squash.' After a while he turned the lamp down to a thin circle and said: 'Go to sleep.'

Next moment he, not she, appeared to have fallen asleep, his cheek, rather rough, against her forehead. Not shivering any more she lay awake listening to his quiet breathing, considering, not for the first time, with amusement mixed with tenderness the capacity of men for falling fast asleep at crucial moments. After half an hour perhaps he stirred, sighed heavily. She drew his face down to kiss him.

'Anny-moan,' he said in a teasing voice, 'are you feeling better?'

'Much better, darling Johnny. Are you?'

'Oh yes. I didn't mean to drop off, though. I meant you to. Sorry.'

'That's all right. It felt nice. But isn't this extraordinary?'

'I suppose it is.'

'To fall through a hole in space, thinking: "This is all a nightmare. I shall wake up soon," and land up – in your arms.'

'It seems to me quite natural.' He turned over lazily towards her. 'How are your poor feet?'

'They seem to have stopped itching.'

'Good. And stop now about holes in space and nightmares and being alone. You're not alone any more, see? Or having morbid dreams or seeing ghosts. If I may say so, you seem to me a very charming person. Not at all spookishly inclined or down in the mouth. Great fun, and very attractive.'

'Thank you,' she said fervently, hugging him, heartened by this image of herself as up to any lark and worthy of pre-war gallantry. 'That's just what I've been trying to explain. The moment I saw you I began – to get a foothold.'

'The moment *I* saw *you* I began to think about – well, this sort of possibility!'

'You didn't, did you! Did you *really*?'

'Oh yes, really and truly, you silly silly girl.'

Presently he added, in a different, stilted voice: 'Not that I could see much future in it.'

She ventured: 'I don't want to seem spooky, but actually I saw you before I came that first time with Ellie to pay you a visit. Do you believe that?'

'If you say so. Though I don't know what you mean.'

He stirred as if uneasy; or bored perhaps with mystifications; so she added lightly: 'I'll tell you another time.'

'Yes do.' He gave her an encouraging kiss.

'Anyway, you looked wonderful. May I go on talking?'

'If you really must.'

'I really must. You can't imagine the relief after all these throttled weeks. It's about – Sibyl. How could I ever have imagined finding her again here? – I mean, that she came here, of all places, to end her days?'

'It is rather rum, I agree: that is, if you and your family were so mixed up with her as you make out.' He stifled a yawn. 'She didn't come here to *die*, you know. It was the last thing she wanted, or intended. It was a shame.'

'I'm sure the last thing she intended was to leave you. I expect she planned to be immortal. Do you know, I remember that blue cape you sometimes have across your knees. Wasn't that hers?'

He said quickly: 'My legs are apt to get chilly. Bad circulation. Yes, that was hers. Her old campaigner's cloak she called it.'

He was smiling to himself. She loosened her clasp of him and turned on her back, listening intently, fearfully, defiantly, and yet with a sense of wishing to placate, apologise, for some sign of Mrs Jardine. But there was no tremor, no rumour of her presence. She was alone with him.

'Johnny, do you believe that – after people die they go on living?' Seeing his suspicion of another approach to the case of his relationship to Mrs Jardine, upon which he intended never to be drawn, she hurried on: 'Miss Stay is certain that death is only a change of consciousness, that everyone goes on – animals as well. She says she's proved it by direct experience. She seems mad, like everyone else here except you. And yet – '

'She's not mad,' he interrupted firmly. 'Cracked, bonkers, barmy if you like. Not mad at all. Actually I'd be inclined not to rule out what she says.'

'How strange. Nobody I know seems to believe it.'

'Perhaps your friends are very clever.' She was uncertain whether or not he spoke sarcastically.

'Ellie thinks Miss Stay is a sort of saint.'

'Ellie has reason to think so.'

'And you?' she asked diffidently. 'You have reason to think so?'

Silence. Then brusquely: 'She believes she can restore me.'

'What part of you?'

He laughed; but his voice had an edge of bitterness. 'Oh! the whole of me. Restore me whole again. One day I shall take up my bed and walk. That is what she thinks.'

'I suppose she knows you can?'

'Oh, that's not her department! That's routine medical stuff – massage, swimming, therapy, exercises, what have you. And plenty of *pluck* and *grit*. And patience, patience . . . No, no, there's to be a miracle. She sees me in my *true body*, you must understand – '

'That's what – ' she stopped herself with a gasp.

'She doesn't,' he went on, 'permit herself to be discouraged by the abject shambling efforts of this – thing you're lying beside.'

'Don't, don't miscall yourself! You are so beautiful. You didn't shamble. You walked upright.'

He held her more closely, as if in gratitude; and when he spoke next, he sounded content again, at ease. 'That tree was a help. I can't think what came over me to show off like that. It was a try-on. The idea came to me – ' He stopped.

'When?'

'When we were swimming, I suppose. You looked so – I wanted to make you smile. I like the way you smile.'

'When you surged up and kissed me? No wonder I smiled.'

'I wanted to follow it up. Ridiculous.'

'Not ridiculous. Wonderful. The wonderful surprise! – I never shall forget it. From then on, everything was magical. Still is.'

All turned now to kissing, to murmured intimate exchanges, to sighs and muffled laughter; but after a while he flung his head back on the pillow; and when she put a hand up and touched his cheek, she felt it wet.

'Johnny, you're not sad, are you?'

'Not really. Pretty happy really. But I wish I'd met you years ago, when I was some use.'

'Oh darling no, it wouldn't have done at all. For one thing, in your heyday I was a clumsy blushing idiotic flapper, too fat – you never would have looked at me. And even supposing you had, I'd have been too dazzled to cast my eyes in your direction. I must have seen your photograph. All you pilots looked like gods, you most of all, I should imagine.'

'Don't be silly.' He sounded not displeased.

'You would have made me miserable. Jealous of dozens of other bowled-over ninepins. I never could bear competition.' She thought about the images of falling heroes – laughing, erotic, doomed, irresistible – only a blur of faces in her adolescent memory. 'I wonder, did you ever come across the Baron? – the Red Baron?'

'I did. In several dog fights. I was so near him once, almost as near, not quite, as you and I are now. We took a long look at one another, a good hard stare. He waved and sort of smiled. Very rum. It wasn't long after that that someone finally got him.'

'What did he look like?'

'Very handsome bloke. Not exactly a reassuring type. Staring eyes. Dismal, fanatical sort of expression.'

'Like Satan in *Paradise Lost*.'

'I'm not very well up in *Paradise Lost*. If you want to know if I dropped flowers on his grave, the answer is I did not. He'd personally shot down two of my best friends.

I wanted to get him. But something went wrong. I didn't.'

'You mean,' she ventured, 'at the last moment you couldn't?'

'I don't know, I don't know,' he said almost angrily. 'Something happened. I might tell you some time: or I might not.' He went on in the same clipped voice: 'If you want to know why I'm living on, the answer is the devil only knows. I don't.'

'How glad *how* glad I am you're living on.'

'Well, I'm not sorry, just at this moment.' Again she felt the upsurge of complex pressure in him – rage, frustration – die away, as it had done, just as startlingly, mysteriously, earlier in the night. A coaxing, caressing, rather shy and boyish person lay beside her, kissing her with ardour. But after a while, as if the words he had used in another context had sparked off a collapse of energy, desire, it was clear that something had gone wrong. He fell away from her on to his back saying petulantly: 'We talked too much.' Then after a strangled silence: 'I wanted to make love to you, properly. I suppose you think I'm incapable.'

'*Of course* I don't think so, darling.' She added, laughing: 'It's been perfectly obvious you're not.'

'But you did think so,' he insisted.

'I never thought so. Not for one moment. Quite the contrary.'

He said, with a huge despondent sigh: 'It's a long time since I've had a girl in my bed.'

'Poor love. Don't worry. There's nothing to worry about. Look, it's getting light, I shall have to go. But I'll come again, and it will be wonderful – we can make love all night. Would you like that? Tonight?'

'Yes,' he muttered. 'But – '

It was her turn to say: 'Go to sleep.'

He muttered: 'Are you all right?' – and almost at once fell into sleep again, as if peacefully exhausted.

When, presently, she left his side, he uttered a faint, protesting, childlike sound, but did not wake. In the breaking light of dawn his face looked so remote, austere, that her heart contracted with a hitherto unknown pang. He seemed to her untouchable; as if withdrawn into a lightless realm, among the shades and ruins of his massacred generation; too far for present human love to reach him.

But throughout next day – and all the days to come – that taste of joy remained, prevailing over the turbulences of the preceding hours: the apprehensions, the nervous, part incredulous, part eager and delighted explorations into sexual intimacy; running like an electric thread, flashing at odd moments through the day's broken texture: the morning bathe; an expedition with Trevor to the store where, from among great bales of dramatically printed cotton (stamped Made in Manchester but never seen adorning native forms) she bought dress lengths for friends and relations; bought also rolls of cotton wool in which to pack her shells and coral pieces; then drinks with the Cunninghams at sunset – Ellie a little depressed, preoccupied – or was it one's guilty fancy? – the Captain addressing Bobby more assiduously, mock-savagely than usual. Even that phenomenon, that nocturnal Apparition, Voice, Visitor, had dwindled in recollection before one moment's piercing, abstract certainty. There it was: one buoyant drop of insubstantial substance, breaking upon her inner firmament with the penetrative radiance of a star newly become visible, traveller from millions of light years' spatial distance. Something entirely separate from human nature's daily food. Something once-known – but when? forgotten, recognised again – but how?

The true taste of love, perhaps.

*

All that day Johnny was invisible. When, at intervals, she cast her eyes in the direction of the hut, it had a look of having been vacated. The boat was gone; no sign of Louis either. A deep qualm shook her. The tree had a menacing appearance, as if stonily encroaching upon a deserted human dwelling place. Towards evening the air became more and more oppressive, impossible to breathe. Colours drained away. The sea heaved, as if about to boil over, beneath its livid surface. A storm was gathering, no doubt of that. Ellie got up and strained her eyes anxiously through the frame of greenery cut by the Captain to command the beach. Presently her frown relaxed.

'That's all right,' she muttered. 'Louis would never risk . . .'

In truth the boat could be seen gliding towards land. The visitor joined her, and they stood side by side in silence, watching the movements of two puppet figures on a dimly painted background. The oars were shipped, Louis was discernible, hauling on the chain until the boat, with Johnny in it, had been pulled well up towards the hut. They turned away. Ellie said abruptly:

'It's sad dear, almost your last evening: I thought we might have . . . But we're in for a nasty storm, Harold said so at lunchtime. I've felt mouldy all day and Harold's got a little black dog sitting on his shoulder. My head! – it's fit to burst – what about yours? You won't be frightened will you, if the thunder and lightning get very bad? I'd be happier if I knew you were safe with Staycie before the rain comes. Tropical rains are solid as a wall, no joke to be caught in. Thank goodness it's come tonight and not tomorrow to spoil our farewell party. Oh how I'm going to miss you! There! – that's the first rumble. Hurry, dear.'

She hurried, pausing half-way up the rock steps for a backward look towards the bay; but her prospect was impeded by the grove of palms. They too looked sinister, leaning starkly this way and that, their crowns like shaggy decapitated heads of monsters stuck on poles.

Princess came wandering towards her, carrying her lamps early, by Miss Stay's instructions, to the Cunninghams. She stopped to announce in a murmur, a happy event in a week's time: the christening of her younger infant daughter.

'And if you please I have select you for her Godmammy.'

'What a compliment, Princess! But soon I go away.'

'That not make matter. You give her nice present yes? before you go away?'

'What shall I give her?'

She deliberated sombrely; then said with a nod towards her victim's wrist: 'Bracelet.'

'No. I want it myself.' It was an antique gold chain bracelet with a heart of pearls and turquoise for its clasp – a present from Anon. 'Why should I give it to you?'

'So when I see it,' muttered the girl, 'I still will think on you.'

Could there possibly be a faint element of true feeling in this preposterous suggestion?

'I tell you what I'll do: I'll find a bracelet in England for your baby, and send it to you.'

Princess stood silent. A kind of film came over the full polished blackness of her eyes. Tears? Sulks? She hung her head.

'Shall I write her name on it? What are you going to call her?'

'Like you. I name her like you. Like Mistress Cun'ham say: No Name.'

'You mean – Anemone?'

'Yes, like I say. No Name.'

She glided on, not smiling.

*

At the top of the verandah steps Miss Stay awaited her, crying: 'Run, run, run! All my little chickabiddies, run for shelter. Mr Bartholomew has just returned – his pilgrimage has quite refreshed his spirit. What a difference! – it's a mortal treat to see it. Only one wee hurdle: the man was set on taking Daisy for an evening gallop; but the Lord be praised I managed to turn his thoughts. She has had her feed, poor patient animal. Tell me now, down in the bungalow, the dear ones all serene? Suffering an evening tête à tête for once I fancy – ' She broke off, sensing something unfortunate somewhere in the phrase; continued with an unfocused look of dream: 'Mysterious are His ways, no doubt of that.'

'You mean the Captain's?'

Miss Stay flung back her head with a crow of wild approval. 'You rogue, you take me up too quick! There's no denying the words could well apply to both beloved parties.' She heaved a sigh; her tone altered to one of solemnity compounded with evasiveness; transfixing the visitor with a ferocious spasm of the eyeballs, she continued: 'Yes . . . yes . . . Someone was on the way. Over and over again I saw it in the cards as clear as clear . . . clear-hidden I should say, but no mistaking. Throwing a long shadow forward.'

'Who was throwing a long shadow forward?'

'You were,' Miss Stay pronounced, for once without equivocation. 'No need to open such great startled eyes. Long rays cast long shadows . . . at the point of intersection. And that is out of our hands. What changes, eh? since you landed on this doorstep, a poor lost slip of an orphan of the storm.'

'Yes, oh yes.' The visitor hung her head and blushed. 'Changes for me, at least.'

'Like a broken lily on its stem,' murmured Miss Stay, pursuing her own train of thought; which, to deflect, the other ventured:

'What *is* happening? I don't quite know.' It sounded feeble.

'Lawks a mercy me! this is none of I!' cried Miss Stay, surprisingly.

'Well, yes, you could put it like that. Perhaps this is an enchanted isle, like Prospero's. Perhaps I shall wake up soon.'

'Oh, there is magic about – strong stuff – no doubt of that. Our visitors often remark upon it. *Be not afraid*, however . . . Oh, I can hear that thrilling voice of hers! We had our fill of culture, our readings from the Bard! She was a liberal education in herself. To think it was you who brought her back! – brought her along with you, all unbeknownst. But you would always be quite a catalyst, I fancy?' She chuckled. 'Surprising, is it not, such grand words falling from these lips! Can you guess who was at pains to tackle our vocabularies? – not least your humble servant's despicable contributions.'

'Yes I can guess. She never could resist a chance of improving everyone.'

'Oh, she was a dab hand at that! But it was highly necessary – and enjoyable to boot – though when it came to the Bard, Mr Bartholomew could cap her on occasion. *He* misses her too – that is, when a faint chord of memory is struck at random . . . Ah! here comes the rain and no mistake. Rain is unusual at this time of year. Who can be the Rainmaker among us? I accused poor Mr Bartholomew, by way of a joke, of course. But he was quite offended. He thought I was referring to his little trouble. He is a sensitive man.'

'His little trouble?'

'Weakness of bladder, dearie, we all come to it. Dear me! what goings-on out there beyond the reef. What a display!' In truth, apocalyptic hieroglyphs in aching violet were zigzagging at rapid intervals down the lowering horizon. 'Let us pray that no ship is struck.'

She peered in the direction of the hut. 'He is safe indoors, I trust.'

'Yes, we saw the boat come back before I left the bungalow.'

'Ah, they will be hobnobbing then, according to their fancies.' She looked pensive. 'All the same, that blessed chap will miss his evening dip. Then he gets blue. With a man, when moodiness sets in, we all know what is apt to follow. 'Tis a mortal shame.' She seemed to leave a question in the air.

The rain was now so loudly crashing and drumming on the verandah roof that the visitor was obliged to shout. 'Will it go on like this? What had I better do?' The head of Miss Stay jerked in her direction. 'I was going to – he asked me to pay him a visit this evening. Perhaps he won't expect me now?'

'Certainly he will! Certainly he is expecting you. Imagine disappointing the blessèd lonely fellow! Slip along down as soon as there's a break. Take my torch, you will find it in the cupboard in the lounge. I must hie me and have an eye to the shutters.' Over her shoulder she called back: 'Don't trouble to return the torch tonight.'

The tremendous wink which accompanied these last words was doubtless due to malfunctioning of the reflex mechanism.

She took the torch, hurried into a swim suit and over it her kimono, and ran out into the cataclysmic downpour, not waiting for the promised break. When she reached the hut, she was sopping, saturated, streaming. He burst out laughing, partly with relief at her arrival, partly at sight of her grotesque appearance. Moving slowly but quite easily about the room while she stripped, he brought her his big towelling dressing gown, wrapped her in it, drew her on to his lap and went on rubbing her down. But her hair was soaking his shirt, and she peeled it off and twisted it into a turban round her head.

'How do I look?' she whispered against his ear.

All this time he had not said a word. She seemed to catch glimpses of him from limitless distances, and at the same time piecemeal, magnified; seeing only his eyes blazing on her, closing, opening; his lips, his hands, his flushed cheek, the dramatic outline of his head and neck when, turning for a moment, he moved a lamp beside them.

Presently they were lying on his bed. Rain rustled and chattered in the sea-grape tree, poured with a voice like a waterfall from the steep-angled roof, driving his house of shells down, down as if into some subaqueous chamber made of echoes, whispers, gleams and shadows, where, clasped together, plunged into one another's being, they were swept again and again through drowning surges; to be thrown up at last into the fertile shallows of a spent flood tide.

Some time after midnight she floated back into conscious separation and awareness, and noticed that the rain had stopped. Sliding out of his arms, she opened the shutters on a night of ineffable fragrance and luminosity, so clear that the moon's whole disk was visible in outline, with only one thin sliver of it stripped – a tilted, silver sickle caught in a net of stars.

He was awake and smiling lazily when she came back to lie beside him. The turban had long ago fallen off, and her hair stood up all over her head in a riot of damp curls.

'Maenad,' he said, gazing at her with brilliant eyes.

She said: 'I'm famished. I had no supper. I came in such a hurry.'

'You don't say! You'll have to forage. There is some

wine in the freezer – we might drink that? and Louis
whipped up something or other for you – knowing you're
always hungry.'

'He really did?'

'He really did. He's fond of you. He calls you Mistress
Nanomee.'

'And Princess thinks I'm No Name. Her baby is to be
christened No Name in my honour. So I shall leave a
little legend in the island. Poor child! – it sounds like a
sad bad story, doesn't it?' But she remembered suddenly:
I have no name, I am but two days old. Joy is my name.

'You won't be forgotten,' he said. 'They do still make
up stories here: very strange ones, Louis tells me.'

'You,' she said, 'will certainly become a legend. You
will always be remembered.'

All at once she was harrowed by a moment's prevision
of his fate: how he would figure in the island's folklore
long after he, the true Johnny . . . . She lay down again beside him, clasping him close, in a passion of regret for his
foreseen, eternal absence from the images of time.

'The Great White Cast Up Man Fish,' he said. 'And
his Virgin Bride – that's you.'

Although he spoke so lightly, the part he allotted to her
startled her: as if the very extravagance of his fantasy
had enabled him, so chary of emotive words, to reach
down to a level where they still lived and resonated
unambiguously. The words 'Virgin', 'bride' went on tol-
ling in her ears; she listened to them, silent, feeling suddenly depressed.

'What's the matter?' he said presently. 'Don't you
fancy it?'

'I do fancy it.'

'You're not crying, are you?' – as if saying: not *again*.

'No. But – '

'But you're not happy?' He sounded nervous, appre-
hensive.

106

'Very, *very* happy. This is the most wonderful, incredible night of my life.'

'But – ?'

'No "buts". I mean you're a perfect lover. Simply remarkable for one so out of practice as you say you are.'

He said with a sigh: 'Well, you're wonderful too.'

He sounded both gratified and grateful; and again the sense of his youth, of the boyishness that lingered in him struck her.

'I think,' she said, 'I was wondering if you really wished I was – what you said just now.'

'What did I say just now?'

'Well, not your bride, that would be very forward of me,' she said, half laughing, half confused. 'I mean the other thing.'

He hesitated. 'Ah . . . that would be old-fashioned of me wouldn't it? He also sounded shy.

'Well, I wish it,' she said passionately. 'If you knew how much I *haven't* enjoyed this, sometimes. I've thought there must be something wrong with me. Perhaps I've never really been in love before. I love you, Johnny.'

As if it was a difficult admission wrung out of him against his will he said: 'Hush. I love you back.'

'What are we to do?'

He muttered: 'I don't know. Stop thinking.'

This time his embraces were so violent, almost savage, that again he seemed a stranger; and when he fell away from her he was breathless, pale with a waxen pallor, the sweat running in rivulets off his face, his neck, his great smooth torso.

Presently she put an ear to his heart and listened to its beat.

'Johnny, your heart is thumping awfully fast and loud.'

He laid a hand quickly on his chest and said:

'It's perfectly all right.' The touch of roughness in his voice surprised her. She sat up and looked down at him.

Smiling, but cold, he said: 'I'm not going to have a heart attack if that's what you suspect.'

She said lightly: 'No, don't. It would be too embarrassing. What would Louis say? And Ellie? And Miss Stay? The imagination boggles.'

'Staycie would say it was all for the best and a blessèd way to go.' His tone matched hers. Still lightly, he added: 'She doesn't anyway expect me to make old bones.'

Her sense of slight malaise persisting, she left his side and went to forage in the kitchen, returning with fruit and Louis's chocolate and mocha whip and a bottle of white wine which, having uncorked, he drank thirstily, saying: 'Excellent, château bottled. Wonder where it's been lurking. Jackie unearthed a dozen the other day and brought them down. Very kind of her. You didn't know I had a cellar, did you?'

She guessed from whom the dozen had originated. She did not wish to dwell on Jackie.

'Delicious whip too,' she said. 'Where is Louis, by the way?'

'Having a night off. Gone to visit his girl friend – one of them.'

'Has he got a girl friend? He's eighty, isn't he? – or ninety?'

'*Mon Dieu, cela n'empêche pas*, in Louis's case.'

'How splendid.'

His French accent was impeccable. She remembered that Mrs Jardine had seen to that, and to his command of the language during his long months in her hospital. She burst out:

'Oh! – I wish she'd go away. Do you feel she's near you sometimes? – hanging around here? Well, she is.'

He set his glass down carefully and filled it again; said nothing.

'So you do know! She was in love with you, wasn't she? – madly madly in love. You were the last, I suppose.

Did you come after one called Gil? Did she ever talk about him? He was killed. I met him once, he kissed me.'

'And now,' he said, 'you've met me and I've kissed you.'

'Don't talk like that! Tell me, were *you* in love with her?'

'Of course not.' A quick bright flush suffused his face. 'If you mean did I make love to her, or want to, the answer is of course not.'

'But she wanted you to.'

'Well, not actually, I suppose.' He sounded awkward, boyishly embarrassed, but not rigidly constrained as heretofore whenever rumour of Sibyl Anstey weighed the air. 'It was bad luck for her, I suppose, to grow old and – and still feel young. I did love her, you know. I owe her so much, as I've told you before. And of course in a way she was still a beauty. Considering her age she could look stunning. And liked to be told so.'

Considering her age . . . Saddest of reservations for a woman. She felt a pang for Sibyl Anstey, the young beauty of her day.

'Yes,' she said. 'Poor Sibyl. I remember her once saying: "the fatal gift of beauty". It's strange how often it's a curse. She must always have been hoping – and expecting – it would be proved otherwise.'

'It was partly my fault,' he said, with a show of compunction.

'How?'

'Well . . .' He stretched himself lazily, grinned. 'I like flirting, and she liked it too. She flirted charmingly. Some elderly ladies do.'

'I dare say.' Her voice was sharp. 'A *divine* game for two, tremendous fun – except perhaps for onlookers: a person's husband say, or daughters, or granddaughters. It used to infuriate Maisie, I remember.'

One eyebrow shot up, he glanced at her, his grin of private amusement fading. He said mildly:

'I don't think old Maisie took it amiss – we got on very well.'

'Oh, I'm sure, I'm sure! I'm sure she adored – adores – you too. Who wouldn't?'

'My darling, what are you going on about?'

The endearment, for the first time on his lips and in his most beguiling voice, melted her mood. He was holding his arms out and she flung herself into them.

'I don't know. I'm frightened. Can I be jealous? When you talk about her you make me feel – outside some inner circle, lonely. She had so much of you. And I've got to leave you here, with all her relics round you, her roof to cover you, all the memories.' With an effort she got out: 'I want her exorcised.'

There was no reply. She raised herself on one elbow to look at him. He smiled at her sweetly, sleepily; said vaguely: 'Don't worry about all that.' He sighed, and swept a glance around the room. 'I've told you before it doesn't feel quite real. I don't belong here. Sometimes I get awfully low.'

With this admission, he laid his head on her shoulder in a gesture of such complete surrender that her very soul seemed pierced with tenderness, contrition. She told herself: 'He trusts me'; and waited, stroking his forehead, for him to speak again.

'I have foul moods – vile. I long to be shot of the whole bloody lot – even Staycie, even Louis. As for that de Pas, I dream of shooting him – and Jackie too. I hate her. I dream they've all died off or shrivelled up . . . and I'm left stranded, chewing seaweed – perhaps a squid or two. What *on earth* am I doing, stuck among these lunatics?' He uttered a sound part laugh part groan, and rolled over on his back, staring at the ceiling. 'Have you noticed how her mouth's twisted?'

'Whose?'

'Jackie's. It used not to be like that – though it was

never an interesting feature. I don't suppose I really hate her. She's not a bad girl. Damn good nurse. Wiry. Popular in the ward, quite a sense of humour. Can you *imagine* getting myself into this situation? – out of sheer – chucking my hand in, not giving a curse what happened to me – handing over lock stock and barrel to her – I mean, our mutual friend. Sheer gutlessness. Despair, if you like.' He leaned across her to take a cigarette from a box on the table, lit it, inhaled once or twice before continuing in a quiet flat voice: 'Before I fell out of the sky there was a girl I'd got engaged to.'

'I thought there must have been. What was her name?'

'Her name was Sylvia in point of fact.'

'Tell me more about her.'

'Sweet girl. Very young. Jolly pretty. Fair hair, blue eyes.'

'She broke it off?'

'Not she. I broke it off. As if I'd have let her tie herself for life to a bloody-minded wreck. That's what she had in mind: she was one of those sacrificial girls. I put paid to all that by wedding my nurse, with Sybil's blessing. *Mariage blanc*, I hope I needn't tell you. And then I agreed – I *agreed* to let myself be shipped far far away to tropic shores, where we could live out our idyll out of reach of any possible interested party.'

'Including your family? – your parents?'

'Yes, my parents. Charming people. I was very fond of them, they're both dead now. I couldn't stand seeing any of them, or letting them see me: pretending they weren't embarrassed, or shattered, or sorry for me. I've got a sister – nice outdoor girl. She married during the war and he was killed, of course. I do hear from her occasionally. She lives in our old home in Cumberland and breeds Jack Russells. Monica, her name is.'

'You don't hear from Sylvia?'

'No, I do *not*. She got married and had some children.

All as it should be.' His hand moved towards his chest, as if to touch the medallion that generally hung there; but he had taken it off. 'I know where she lives,' he added. 'I used to have a beastly dream of walking up to her front door and opening it and looking for her. But I never could find her, she was always just out of sight. That's all over. It belongs to another life – finished; *nothing*.'

'You did love her very much?'

'Thinking about her tonight, I wonder. I thought I did, of course. But why should I think about her tonight? Perhaps,' he suggested, 'it's not very flattering to you?'

'You are silly, darling. If one's thinking about love, as you are perhaps, one's bound to think about all the people one has loved.'

'Jolly few, in my case – I don't know about you. Don't tell me.' He kissed her affectionately, but absent-mindedly. 'Is that it? Perhaps it is. That's where Sibyl came in. She was my anaesthetic. What I'd have done without her . . . She invented a whole new life for me – a proper, going concern. She put so much energy into it . . . And I think it was – what's the word? – disinterested. She knew what she was looking for, and she set about finding it: a place where I could live outdoors mostly, and reconstitute my framework. No swimming pool stuff – big swimming. She scoured the coasts of the world. If you remember her you'll know how practical she was and thorough.'

'Oh yes, I do remember. That was one of the reasons why children felt so safe with her.'

'Yes. I felt safe,' he said musingly, with a faint wry smile. 'Like all her schemes, it was magnificent. But it had a flaw in it. Three flaws, you might say.'

Echoes assailed her of almost the same words, a similar theme, to which she had listened long ago.

'Her, me, Jackie,' he continued, 'the equation: that's what she didn't manage to get right.'

'She never did. But then, who does? Did everyone get

into a frightful muddle?'

He considered. 'I wouldn't say that. Jackie anyway shook it all off. It wasn't me that ever troubled Jackie, it was Sibyl: she had a crush on her. But she got over it in time. She's not one to pine; she's a resourceful girl: she settles for what's available.'

'That left two of you.'

'I didn't quite – ' he began to speak disjointedly. 'She was such marvellous stimulating company, and old enough to be – I never could understand why she should bother about me. I'm not in the least brainy, I'm simply average, ordinary – '

'But simply beautiful.'

He gave her a slight impatient shake, as if, perhaps, to say he had heard that often enough; or as if some disturbing chord of memory had been touched. She could hear the syllables vibrate in Mrs Jardine's throat. She added:

'And she simply fell in love with you, poor Sibyl. Oh, how glad I am I wasn't there. She would never have let you make love to me.'

After a tense pause he got out: 'I couldn't *possibly* have . . . Unthinkable. Apart from her being old – and ill as well – I sort of put her on a pedestal. It would have been like violating – Well, I don't know.'

'But that's not how she saw it.' She hesitated. 'I see – I do see how it seemed to her.'

'How did it seem?' he said rather sulkily.

'Well . . . Making you whole again, which was her job, meant – as she saw it – loving *her* exclusively. Being restored meant being her perpetual captive.'

'I never counted on being what you call restored – never even began to count on it. In the beginning I was much more helpless than I am now. Besides – '

'You thought you'd never be able to make love again.'

'I was sure I was done for – impotent.' He heaved a

huge sigh and gave her a quick kiss. 'Not that we ever actually discussed it, but – ' he sighed again, 'it got rather embarrassing sometimes, knowing she was – oh Lord! – making herself – you know – seductive, sort of . . .'

'Oh dear . . .' He had delicate feelings, he was chivalrous. Unlike some people . . . He leaned across her to stub out his cigarette, fell back again and said:

'I killed her.'

'What do you mean?' But it was as if he had said it in the first moment of their meeting; or as if she had all along been waiting for the moment of his saying it.

'I do *not* mean I took an axe to her, or strangled her.'

He brooded, and to encourage him she enquired:

'Was it her heart? I remember her propped up with pillows, her lips blue, and somehow getting the idea from Maisie she might die any moment – from a sudden shock.'

'That's it. The moment came. And Maisie. And the shock.'

Again it all seemed about to become the beginning of a once familiar story.

'A shock she died of?'

'Not on the spot. But – yes.'

'I see, I see. You got on well – too well – with Maisie.'

'It was all right in the beginning. Everybody happy. She was so wrapped up in that kid of Maisie's; and so proud of Maisie being a doctor. But then . . . You may remember, Maisie's a free and easy convivial sort of bloke. And Sibyl started to get suspicious.'

'Of anything in particular?'

'Well, we liked sitting up late. And drinking.'

'Ah, Sibyl wouldn't approve of that. She'd think that very vulgar. Also she would deplore what sitting up late and drinking leads to.'

'That was just the trouble,' he said, with simple if rueful amusement. 'We got sort of amorous. Nothing serious. You might not think it to look at her, but the doctor's quite game for a romp. And she didn't mind that I wasn't any good. She's a kind old bag.'

'She helped restore your manly confidence.'

'Perhaps she did. Don't be so beastly sarcastic.'

'It all sounds to me very vulgar. I'm on Sibyl's side. I don't care for romps.'

'Oh, you don't!' He hugged her, teased her, laughing silently, perfectly relaxed.

'And I doubt if Maisie's motives were altogether pure. Though of course that wouldn't bother you.'

'Oh, you *are* cross! Why are you? One thing I do promise you: she's not nearly, not *nearly* as attractive as you. Not really my type.'

'That is good news. But stick to the point. This is supposed to be a deadly serious confession. What happened?'

'O-o-oh!...' He let out a prolonged groan and sank into depression. 'What happened was: in the early hours, there was Sibyl suddenly, in the doorway. Glaring, shaking. We thought Louis had carried her up hours ago. But it seems she'd told him to leave her, that Maisie was going to see to her. She said she'd been calling for hours, that she needed whatever it was she took for her palpitations, that she'd been deserted. She cried, it was terrible, she collapsed on the floor, and sobbed and sobbed. She said it was the *bitter shame* – her own granddaughter no better than a trollop. And one of the most revolting crimes was abuse of hospitality.'

'What did that mean?'

'Using her precious sacred house for immoral purposes. Actually,' he said, suddenly becoming a caught-out, self-justifying schoolboy, 'we were only drinking and smoking, thank the Lord – and playing the guitar. But it was unpardonably squalid according to her standards.'

He paused; went on despondently: 'From first to last she never looked at me. Maisie picked her up and carried

her all the way back to the house. She was almost unconscious. Just before dawn she died . . . Maisie holding
her hand.' He added in a strangled voice: 'That was the
last I saw of her. I don't think she forgave me.'

'I'm sure she did. Of course she did. She loved you –
and she always forgave. She was magnanimous.'

'Yes. Well, I hope so. She sent me an odd sort of
message. Actually, the last thing she said.'

'What was it?'

'Something about a slayer. *O young man o my slayer* . . .
that was it. She said: "Tell him it's a quotation", and
she smiled, according to Maisie – a real smile. You
remember her smile? – enormously amused.'

'I do. And her tears. I remember both.'

She lay back, straining her ears as if to catch the echo
of a voice. 'And I remember one of the last things she
said to *me*.' She paused and he turned his head enquiringly.
'That you don't want to be – saved.'

'Oh, saved?' Disgusted voice. 'But what on earth – I
don't know what you're getting at.'

'Never mind. I felt she had come to warn me off. You
were her property and trespassers would be prosecuted –
that was the feeling she conveyed. But I dare say it was
just my guilty conscience. You know how it works in
dreams.'

'Oh, this dream you're so mysterious about . . . To
hell with that. But if you somehow picked up the idea
that I won't be *anybody*'s property you were spot on.'

'Yes, I picked up the idea. What about Staycie? She's
after saving you as well,' you told me.

'That's different.'

'You mean she doesn't want to go to bed with you.'

He uttered a sound expressive of dismay, and shook her
again. 'Shut up! The old girl means well, bless her heart;
but I'm not a co-operative subject. I just don't fancy it.'

'What don't you fancy?'

'I don't fancy living.' There was a long silence which he finally broke by murmuring: 'Though tonight it doesn't seem such a bad idea. Not bad. Not bad at all.'

Then again she was gathered into his arms; for the last time he made love to her – this time more tenderly by far, more confidently, considerately. Afterwards he said for the first and the last time: 'I love you.' A few tears mingled with their grateful kisses. Again she asked: 'What are we to do?' This time he answered: 'I don't know yet. I must think.'

Daylight was breaking rapidly. Raising herself on one elbow, hand propped on cheek, she took a long deep look at him. He lay with his head thrown back, eyes half closed, only two narrow glinting curves showing beneath the lids, his expression undecipherable. There was something about it – something severe, as of one rapt in meditation, impersonally triumphant, even majestic, that made her want to catch her breath, as if he dazzled her, or frightened her. A strange, primitive, female experience of worship, of subservience, totally unfamiliar, overcame her. He seemed scarcely to be attentive when she murmured: 'I must go now'; put on his dressing gown, combed her wild hair with his comb, collected her still damp belongings. But then he roused himself, saying 'Listen'; and they had a conversation. He told her to come back around mid-morning: he would have a plan for the day prepared by then. A plan for them to spend the day together? Yes, he said firmly, and mind she fell in with his arrangements. No one, not Ellie, Trevor, Kit, Staycie, Bartholomew, Princess, was to be allowed to balls up this day alone together. They could whistle for her until evening and this damned farewell party. She was to run along now and have a bit of kip. He would do the same. To hear him take charge of her with such authority set the final seal upon her happiness. The day before them seemed to stretch out into eternity.

When she looked back at the door to wave to him he was again lying motionless as an image on a bier, his great torso and long naked limbs lit by the unearthly apricot light of dawn.

When she rejoined him she found him already seated in the stern of a trim motor boat – not Tony de Pas's inferior outboard affair – a boat, he said vaguely, that he could sometimes lay his hands on. Louis, his massive countenance split in an ear to ear grin of amusement and delight, waited to hand her in and to shove the little craft out into deeper water. Oars, two strong sticks, bathing gear, a picnic basket, bottles were stowed in place. Johnny wore a green eye shade, and gave an approving glance to her large becoming hat tied on with a red and white cotton scarf. 'That's right,' he said. 'There's a hell of a glare on the water. You don't want to get sunstroke your last day.'

'Where are we going?'

'To a place I know that nobody else knows. Nobody has been there since the world began. A goodish way beyond the Point. We mustn't go *too* far, must we? It wouldn't do if we ran out of gas and I never got you back: if we broke down and simply drifted on to the reef, and they waited in vain for No Name Anemone Anonyma at her farewell celebrations.'

'I can row,' she said. 'I'm very strong.'

'Let me feel. By Jove yes, what muscles, how absolutely topping! I say Boysie – may I call you Boysie? – isn't this simply ripping?'

He wouldn't stop teasing her, she couldn't stop giggling. He whistled, he steered, they watched the land receding, its conical, densely vegetated hills rising high, higher, like huge waves, viridian, violet, overtopping one another. At one moment some great fish leapt quite near the boat, and he exclaimed excitedly, wishing he had brought a rod. Nothing romantic or intimate was said. Their holiday spirits flowed through one another as if their bodies were transparent: as light-filled, as exhilarated as the blue air and sparkling hyacinthine, amethyst-streaked sea. After rounding the Point they came into choppy water. The breeze was stiff, the boat danced over little foamy white caps. He said: 'There's quite a current here.' Trivial, idly-spoken words . . . but some trick of his voice, of the turn of his head, set going an unaccountable vibration. *I know it all*, she told herself. Blue blazing sky and water, rocking boat; another time, remote, remote; another, once-familiar place; a man's voice drifting on the wind, saying those very words; a nobly proportioned head, dark ruffled hair, a high-bridged nose, full chin seen in profile, a long gold-skinned arm, a powerful-looking hand intent on steering . . . *All as before, as once upon a time*. Nothing charged with drama in the glimpse, nothing intrinsically memorable or significant; simply a momentary, total dislocation, a shock both acute and painless, compounded of accept-ance and astonishment. If she had found words expressing feelings they might have been: 'So it's true, we do know one another very well'; yet there was nothing emotive, nothing ambiguous attached to the clear image.

He was looking at her more attentively.

'You're very silent. Feeling seasick?'

'Certainly not. But getting hungry.'

'Again?!'

'Well, I had no breakfast, not a bite. The storm had got everybody down. The bread was damp, the coffee was stone cold. I didn't see Miss Stay: she went down very early to the bungalow. Mr Bartholomew was fractious. Miss Cropper had a horrible shock – a scorpion fell out of her hairbrush. I hurried to her when I heard her yell, but it gave me the creeps, I couldn't touch it. I called Princess and she banged it and killed it with the hairbrush, looking scornful. I wish I hadn't seen it.'

While she chattered on, he swung the boat round, steering for the shore. It occurred to her while she watched the land approaching, how little she had been affected by the depression and disarray prevalent in the guest house: even the unnerving sight of the scorpion had barely brushed her consciousness, whereas less than three weeks ago it would have appalled her, transfixed her with yet one more symbol of the obscene threats of evil which surrounded her.

The boat grounded gently; she stepped out barefoot into crystal water, the colour of gentians; then steadied the boat while he rolled his slacks half-way to his knees, picked up his sticks, heaved himself out and stood upright, with care, on his long, shapely, wasted legs.

'There!' he said triumphantly. 'The bay that wanted to be visited.'

'It never has been?'

'Never, I told you, since the world began. Once or twice, fishing with Louis, I've spotted it – missed it other times. It seems to hide. It's a present for you, darling. Anonyma Bay on the map.'

It was a deep, shell-strewn scallop of snow-white sand, out of which grew, here and there, a thorny shrub covered with vermilion blossoms and with the huge yellow and black striped butterflies that fed on them. A feathery grove of tall bamboos ringed the beach; and further back, a tumble of dark boulders rose to a towering cliff. Over this a fall of water, at first tenuous and sheer as a scarf of silvery tissue, cascaded downwards, carving a fertile channel, thick with dripping ferns and clumps of arum lilies in its lower reaches.

She pulled the boat up further, collected their gear; and they walked slowly across the virgin sand into the shade of the grove. He lowered himself on to a rock with a scooped-out surface, saying: 'Even a ready-made armchair'; and she spread the canvas sheet and sat at his feet.

They ate and drank – Louis's lovingly packed delicacies washed down with iced rum punch, iced coffee – in happy silence, overcome by the dazzle and somnolence of high noon. Then he stretched himself out beside her, pulled her into his arms and went to sleep. An hour passed. He woke up smiling, kissed her, sat up, looked down at her, one eyebrow lifted.

'No kip?'

'Not quite. I was thinking.' Thinking: only a few more hours together.

'What about? Women never sleep.' He yawned. 'I was strangely sleepy.'

'No wonder.'

'I'd like to make love to you. What's the matter? Why do you look like that?'

'How do I look?'

'Broody. Worried. Are you?'

'Yes. No. Yes. Johnny we must talk – we must.'

'Yes. Well . . . We must. Let's have a swim first.'

He was in bathing trunks under his shirt and slacks. He watched her undress, saying: 'Oh, you are pretty. Why wear that garment? Don't.' But she said: 'I'd better. There's someone watching – look! We aren't the first.'

His head turned with feline swiftness following her pointing finger. Some distance back, in a patch of green grass within the grove, a white cow stood tethered to a mango tree, motionless as if painted on the landscape.

'I'll be damned!' he said. 'Can it be real? Has it been there all the time?'

'I think we've dreamed it up. It looks quite benevolent.'

'It's a cow-goddess, come to bless us.'

He let her help him, one arm around her shoulders, till he was knee-high in the water; then he plunged forward with an almighty splash, surfaced without looking back, drove on, on, on, leaving her lonely, far behind. He was a dot, bobbing, almost out of sight; and the vast expanses of empty sea and sky seemed suddenly to glare at her. Then he was tearing back, all thrashing arms and shoulders and plastered hair and streaming radiant face; swung her into his orbit, taking big breaths to say: 'Come on – arms round my neck – hang on – take you for a ride – no sharks no barracudas – special dolphin rescue technique – more efficient – much more fun.' Carrying her on his back as if the weight of her were nothing, he cruised out to sea again. Eyes closed, arms loosely round his neck, she let herself float onward with his measured, rhythmical, strong strokes. Once or twice he gave a shrug and a laugh and rolled her off his shoulders; then for a while they swam abreast. He played in the water as if it was his natural element, as if he could never tire; bore her along as if he would never let her flag or fall behind.

'What are we doing?' she gasped once. 'Shall we ever get back?'

'I wonder!'

'Are you sure – no sharks or – ?'

'No, no. We're well inside the reef. Anyway nearly all sharks are harmless.'

'You're not going to drown me, are you?'

'I haven't decided.'

He was beside her, not smiling, staring at her. Next moment, clasped in his arms, she let herself sink down with him in a supreme embrace. Then she struggled, and shot rapidly to the surface and found herself alone, looking all round for him, suppressing panic. Long of limb and heavy as he was he came up slowly, as if reluctantly.

'Frighten you?'

'I can't be frightened when I'm with you.'

'But you almost were? You were?' he said in his odd insistent way.

'Well, almost. When I thought you were never coming up.'

'The water's too buoyant,' he said vaguely.

That was the moment when his mood of insouciance, serenity, began to change; though all he said, after a smiling glance at her, was: 'Total immersion. Now you belong to me.' Then: 'I didn't know your eyes were green.'

'They're not.'

'They are. *Bright* green. And icy. You're a mermaid. And oh, how pale you are. You're tired. You've had enough.'

'I'm not tired . . .'

'*Right*! Just as you say. Back now.'

As if in obedience to instructions he turned and started for the shore, his progress slow enough to permit her to keep only a yard or so behind him. But once they were back in the pellucid shallows, and could stand, he paused, frowning, looking all round him as if perplexed or hesitant. He waist-high, she breast-high in the water, they confronted one another. He put a hand beneath her chin and tipped her face up as if to search it closely. His light eyes seemed to hold a shadow, and to cast it over her. He kissed her – another cold salt kiss, then he started to wade for the shore with dragging steps. She hurried forward to fetch his sticks, but he said irritably: 'No – too much trouble'; reached for the boat and tumbled into it. He said: 'Be a good girl and fetch me a cigarette: that's what I'd really like.' When, having dressed in haste, she returned with all their gear he was sitting collectedly in the stern, searching the contours of the land through a pair of binoculars; which presently were offered to her and sulkily refused. He started whistling, continued his

123

geographical survey with every appearance of intent pre-occupation. She busied herself with comb, lipstick, powder, suntan cream, pulled her hat down to hide her chagrined face. In silent estrangement they sat side by side.

'Why,' she said finally, 'do men so enjoy looking through those blasted things?'

'I've never asked myself,' he said mildly. 'Do you object?'

'I'll tell you why: it's because they so hate to look at what's under their noses.'

He briefly laughed, put down the offending object; then said in an altered voice:

'Perhaps I'm beginning – not quite to be able to enjoy looking at you. Because of such a short time left.' At a gesture, an indrawn breath from her he went on coldly: '*Don't cry*. I suppose it's all been a mistake.'

She protested wildly, desperate to force the breakdown of his stony front; and after some time he heaved a hard-drawn sigh, put an arm round her and muttered:

'I didn't mean it to get out of hand.'

'To be so important?'

He nodded.

'But it is?'

'Seems to be.'

'Well, that's all that matters: that it should be important.'

'I don't like being irresponsible.'

She lifted her head from his shoulder to study his serious face. She said:

'You almost startled me. No one has ever said that to me, so far as I remember.'

'Isn't it said any more?' he enquired in that mild tone he sometimes adopted. 'Is it out of date? I live so retired . . .'

'Perhaps I've been unlucky. Unwise, more likely.'

'I don't know anything about your life.'

'Do you want to?'

'If you want to tell me.'

Her past stirred in her, all amorphous, clouded:
nothing in clear narrative sequence emerged; no definite
outlines or solid forms.

'It's not been very interesting or dramatic. Nobody's
ever had reason to be proud of me. I think a lot about
people. Otherwise the only thing I've ever given much
thought to is – ' He looked at her enquiringly; and she
went on, feeling shamefaced:

'Happiness. Personal happiness. That's what I believed
in. That's what I was after.'

'Well – what's wrong with that? Who wants unhappiness?' He sounded kind but cautious.

'Oh! – but to put it in the forefront is disgraceful and
ridiculous. Anyone will tell you it's just a by-product of
– of getting on; or, if you're noble, service to humanity.
I simply wanted a blissfully happy marriage, and lots of
children.'

He reflected. 'It doesn't sound too impossibly ambitious.
. . . It must be what millions of women want, even
today . . . But you don't believe in all that any more?'

'Well, look at me!' He did so, smiling sweetly; and she
went on, the tears running down her face: 'Oh! if you
knew how frightened I am now!'

'Frightened of what?'

'Of – something about my proportions.'

'I see nothing wrong with *them*.'

'Internal, I mean. And I can't alter them.'

'You're not saying you're barmy or something, are
you?'

'You mustn't tease. I used to think the main thing in
everybody's life was love. But it isn't: I found that out
long ago. People can manage with only a pinch of it –
if that. They're not nice people but they function. I

literally can't. I *cannot* live without love: without – you know, being in a state of love. A loved and loving state. Can you?'

'I do,' he muttered. 'I told you. I'm not loving – or lovable.' He hung his head, idly picking at a paint blister on the floor boards.

There was a long melancholy deadlocked silence, which she broke at last to say uncertainly:

'When I arrived here, I was more frightened than ever in my life. *Totally* frightened. Between one moment and the next I'd dropped out of the human situation – as I saw it. I had no future. Apart from despair, I was incredulous. I suppose I'd always assumed that in spite of setbacks I'd – stay on the winning side. I've learnt now what outcasts, exiles feel: that's something to the good, I suppose.'

'Yes,' he said. 'That's something.'

'You know about it too?'

'About what?' His voice was guarded.

'Not being on the winning side.'

'Of course. It's better, safer. One can manage fairly well.' He threw his head back, and the strange cut-off sound, half-groan, half laugh, which she had heard before escaped him. 'But *I'm* not on any side. I don't compete.'

'You mean that you're not greedy . . . I feel that when I'm with you. It makes a nice change.'

'Don't imagine,' he said, more lightly, 'I was putting in a selfless effort to cheer you up last night.'

'And don't *you* imagine I was.'

'Well,' he said contentedly, 'you did cheer me up no end, whatever your intention was.'

'You promise? You weren't – hoping, pretending I was someone else?'

'Don't talk such rubbish,' he said indignantly. 'As if I'd pretend you were anybody else! As if I'd want to!'

'You said it was a long time since – you know – a girl in your bed.'

'So it was. What's wrong with saying that? D'you think any old tart would have done as well? Louis would have combed the islands to bring me a selection if I'd said the word. There's plenty of pretty girls in Port of Spain – black, brown, white, all shades. Oh, what *am* I to do with you? You are so silly.' He shook her; then relenting, patted her. '*Now* what is there to cry about?'

'I'm not. If I were, it would be for happiness.'

'Aha! Happiness is out for keeps, remember.'

But she said soberly: 'What a marvel it is. Simply a marvel. From the first moment of seeing you it started.'

'That evening you got so drunk?'

'I didn't – I wasn't, I never am. *You* were . . .'

He drew her again into light-hearted flirting, teasing her sweetly as if all time was theirs to play in. A double echo pierced her once again: the voice of Ellie, wistful, evoking so much more than she could dream of: '*I used to hear them laughing together. It sounded so nice.*' She spared a thought, unenvious, drained of rancour, perturbation, for Sibyl Anstey, acknowledging, with compassion, her claim to be recognised, respected, in the world which something of Johnny's essential self inhabited; into which she too had now gained entrance: adorable pagan world, ravishing young man, with the god-like gift of laughter preserved intact beneath the shell he had built round himself.

As if catching her train of thought – no more than a kind of shimmer in her mind – he said:

'But you must see I'm extremely resistible. I can't think why you permitted all those liberties.'

'Not with a view to therapy, I promise you – like you know who. I think it was chiefly curiosity – like you in reverse. I wanted to see if I could stop you smiling.'

'Don't you like my smile?'

'It was so formal – it put me in my place. I wanted to see if there was anything – for me – behind it. But I don't mean to criticize your teeth, they're absolutely splendid. A pleasure in themselves.'

He took a pocket mirror from her bag and had a look at them. 'They're OK,' he agreed. 'God knows what I'd do if they started to crumble. Do you think a complete set in gold would be attractive? But you've hurt their feelings. I'll never smile at you again.'

'You won't be able to help it. Oh, darling Johnny! – how can we face Ellie's party? Everyone will see what's happened, it must be obvious. Will Staycie think we look a mortal treat?'

'I shan't be coming to the party.'

In the ensuing pause the future surfaced, menacing, like the snout of a shark breaking through smiling waters.

'No,' she said under her breath. 'No, we couldn't bear it, could we? But how shall I get through it? And Ellie will be so sad.'

'It can't be helped. I'll see quite enough of her after you've gone.'

'After I've gone . . . What will you do?'

'Go on much as usual I suppose. Swim. Play chess. Go fishing. Eat. Drink. Sleep.' With another attempt at lightness, he added: 'Lead a chaste life.'

'Will you miss me?'

He did not reply; swallowed; and after a pause said: 'And you? What about you?'

'You mean, shall I miss you? At the moment I don't see how I can bear to leave you. It seems as if you had become my life.'

He made a quick gesture of negation; then said stiffly:

'That chap you've mentioned – are you – do you still want to marry him?'

She said slowly: 'All I *think* I want now, is to find out why? – what happened? Obliterate the enormous query.

It's been like being blocked by a huge fallen tree that I couldn't move; the torn up roots sticking up in the air like snakes, the earth bleeding and full of dying crawling things. What do you do with a blown-down tree you've known and loved for a long time? You can't replant it. You have to cart it away. I *could not* think how. The very idea seemed too hopeless to conceive. But now . . . I seem to have stepped over it, thanks to you.'

She thought: most of all she would like to look back and see . . . that chap withered, blasted, while she ran off laughing: but Johnny would be shocked by such vindictiveness, perhaps. Indeed he appeared to be striving towards strict impartiality, if not last-ditch masculine solidarity by remarking reasonably:

'I expect you'll forget all that when you see him again.'

'I don't ever want to see him again. Except, as I said, to ask *why*?'

'Well, he'll probably be able to give you a satisfactory answer.'

'Do you *hope* he will?'

He said, with stubborn detachment: 'Oh! . . . what *I* hope he'll say or do! . . . I simply want *you* to be happy.'

Mastering her urge to say querulously: That's no way to talk, she attempted an equal reasonableness.

'What would you call a satisfactory answer? "Some unforeseen crisis arose and I couldn't help myself"? "My wife had a nervous breakdown"? "One of the children broke his leg"? "I found I didn't love you any more"? "I've fallen in love with someone else"? . . . One of these things, or none of them, might be true. Or else that he suddenly had to go abroad – on a job.'

He said with a flicker of curiosity: 'What sort of a job?'

'I don't know. He's a journalist – freelance now; and he's special correspondent for a weekly you wouldn't have heard of. That's what takes him abroad now and then, he says. Sometimes I do wonder what he's up to.

Whether he's in Intelligence.'

'A spy, you think he might be.'

'Some sort. It would fit in with something in his character that mystifies me: his way of looking you particularly straight in the eye, and at the same time making a sort of complicated – verbal – sidestep which only strikes you as odd when you think about it afterwards.'

'A bit unreliable,' he suggested. Then, after a pause: 'Of course I can't possibly judge, but it seems a bit unfortunate that you ever got mixed up with him.'

'I agree,' she said mournfully. 'It was a mistake. I've only myself to blame for making it – and for sticking to it. He always swore – I really thought he meant it.'

'Meant what?'

'That he couldn't do without me. He's a very brilliant man – and attractive – and the opposite of dull. When we first met he was pretty well the top, non-queer, slightly disreputable glamour-boy in circulation. Perhaps you don't realise how scarce they are on the ground these days. Girls have to look around . . . I was very flattered when he fell in love with me. After a time we had rows, but we always made it up. I promised him – he made me promise – to wait till he was free.'

'To marry you, you mean? You were to be married as soon as he was free?'

'That was the idea – was what he said in the beginning. But there was always something insuperable cropping up to prevent him getting free. Then he'd say wait, please wait, trust me – and I did. Then the subject rather faded out . . . and I got into the habit of telling myself it was better as it was – better not to be always together. It made promises and trust and general good behaviour more difficult, so more worth striving for, more – morally important. And then, it meant he wouldn't get bored with me – he's very prone to get bored: that our times of being together would stay vital, and fresh and stimulating. About six months ago he said suddenly: "The elastic's stretching, you know, it's stretching. Soon it will have no stretch." I said, did he mean he was getting sick of me, and the situation? He said no, never, but he felt *I* was withdrawing. I said, nonsense, but the time had come for him – for us, to change the set-up, once and for all.'

'What did that mean?'

'Decide to be together – or decide to part. He said he knew which it must be – we must be together – but I must give him time. He went away and I didn't see him for some weeks but I felt quite calm and confident: can you imagine such idiocy? Then he came back as loving as ever, more so, and said, that was it, he'd burnt his boats, he'd told his wife, he had no doubts. He expounded this beautiful plan . . . It all sounded so solid, so taken care of . . . Then he went away again – for a fortnight. He said he had lots of things to settle. We were to meet – at Bristol! I went on moving like a sleep walker: I see that now, looking back. There was the strangest feeling all the time that nothing was quite real – that I was in a web. You know the rest.' He nodded, looking severe. She added: 'I've come to the conclusion he never intended to get free. It was part of the game – part of the dangerous fun. I expect he was playing it with others besides me: his wife perhaps: God knows who else: someone, or something I don't know about.'

He seemed so sunk in meditation that she asked presently: 'Have you been listening, Johnny?'

'Yes, I've been all ears.'

'What do you make of it?'

He shrugged his shoulders, glanced at her, looked away again: 'Nothing. I make nothing of it.' His voice expressed profound distaste.

'This sort of – rather nightmarish disaster does seem to happen to people nowadays . . . Perhaps we're all in a web.'

'That I can believe,' he said.

'Yes, you said something . . . About millions of people being homesick before long. Is that the sort of thing you meant?'

'More or less. In a sense.'

'And Ellie said: the heart of the world is broken. That's another way of saying it: not *your* way, of course, you have no use for hearts.'

His smile was strained and bitter. He took both her hands and looked at them attentively.

'Well, what am I to do? Tell me.'

'How can I tell you?'

She ventured tremblingly: 'You don't like being irresponsible, you said.'

He said, as if cornered: 'You should get married, I think, and have a family.'

'Oh . . . you think so.'

'Someone boring perhaps, who wouldn't mind you nagging.'

She turned impetuously towards him, grasped him by both shoulders crying his name with desperation. They stared into one another's eyes.

'Sweetheart, no,' he said at last. 'It wouldn't do. How could it? I'm just an accident in time.'

'Don't say that! You're all my meaning now. Don't laugh at me.'

'I'm not – I don't.' His voice sounded strangled.

'Why are we here together? Why did you bring me to this place? What have we been proving, ever since we met?'

He shook his head, as if baffled.

'That we belong together. That we accept all of one another. When I go away I take you with me, I stay here with you, you know that, don't you?'

He nodded, heavily sighed.

'We must think, we must think,' he said: not: 'I must think', as before.

'Besides, I'm going to have a baby.' He stared at her, speechless; and she added roughly: 'Yours of course.'

'How can it be "of course"? How can you know?'

'I don't, but I *do* know. I'm certain. Last night while you were asleep I said to myself: "Now I've started a baby." Didn't it occur to you? It ought to have.' He looked rueful. 'Don't look so worried. It did occur to me. Have you heard of calculated risks? I took one.'

'Oh, you are reckless . . .' He sounded aghast, admiring.

'Are you pleased?'

'Very pleased. I mean, I will be, if – ' The colour, that flush of carmine, showed vivid in his cheeks.

'I told you, it isn't "if". Shall you want me to let you know how I get on?'

'I should jolly well hope so. What do you suppose?' he said indignantly again. Then suddenly his features altered, he looked pinched. 'Were you proposing – what are you proposing?'

'What are you suspecting?' Once more an intimation brushed her, as if from some far back memory or knowledge of a dangerous area contained in him. He lit a cigarette and shot her a look that might have been apology or mistrust. 'That I'll make a shotgun marriage as soon as I get home? You wouldn't like it, would you, if I came hurrying back here, pregnant, to be made an honest woman of?'

'No, not really.' Some private train of thought caused him to shake his head, then shake with a spasm of silent laughter. He took her hand up and said quietly: 'My dear girl, you don't suppose I'd let you go through it by yourself? I shall come to you. I shall come to England.'

'You will?'

'Of course. I shall come and look after you.' He lifted

his head and stared towards the horizon as if, at last, the incentive he had been awaiting had appeared – his face open now, serene, washed with the light's air-and-water radiance. She disengaged her hand and laid it on his heart, imagining – or not imagining – that she could feel its turbulence like an alarum in her breast; scarcely daring to look at him; suppressing her own uprush of wild anticipation, hope, fear . . . sudden anguish.

'Not out of . . . a sense of duty?' she ventured.

'Don't be such an idiot.'

'And you won't suspect I've trapped you?'

He burst out laughing. 'Or the other way round? Let's say we've trapped each other.'

'I was afraid you'd say it must be got rid of.'

'Good God!' He looked quite disgusted.

'I've never had an abortion, but most of my girl friends have.'

'What bad company you keep.'

He half meant it: he was inclined to think such goings-on repellent, squalid. She must be careful not to shock his sensibilities. Her eyes filled, as she looked at him, with happy tears: she saw him not only as the man she loved but as the symbol of a rare, perhaps a disappearing species: a man with uncomplicated sources of sexual pride and confidence. His restored potency delighted him of course: what was unfamiliar in her experience was his simple male pride in, and satisfaction with, the proof of his fertility. Lost in wonder, she told herself that the child was already wanted, welcomed; that she was now esteemed and cherished not only for herself but as the bearer of the child. Next moment he said solemnly:

'Will you marry me, Anonyma?'

'I will.'

Silence.

'Now I must take you back,' he said.

As if at a given signal a wave, then another, another,

running rapidly from nowhere shivered the bay's placid improbable crystal, dissolved against the boat, lifting it free from its bed of sand. 'Quite a commotion,' he murmured. 'Must be a passing steamer.' He started the engine and they glided out to sea. Turning for a last look at the scalloped shore, the bamboo thicket, the waterfall, she saw that another figure had appeared beside the still discernible white cow: a tall slender negro youth, in rags, his head and features sculpturally modelled, motionless, holding, as if it were a ritual staff of office, a long bamboo pole. He seemed to have something on his head, worn casually askew: was it a wreath of leaves and flowers? But the distance widened; next moment this surprising sun-dappled figure had disappeared.

On the return journey, thoughts of Ellie's awful party loomed. She would not, explained Johnny, expect him to be present. It was to be a slap-up all-embracing do: everyone would be there, including Tony de Pas and Jackie and her crew. But round about midnight she was to slip away and come to the hut. He had something to give her. After that, he and Louis would start off on a fishing expedition, in a proper boat with oars. He would be gone all night, probably next day. Midnight would strike farewell.

'But not goodbye for long, Johnny? You do mean it. We're not mad, are we?'

'I do mean it, we're not mad.'

'But supposing – '

'Supposing nowt. Just wait. Trust me. I'll be coming.'

'We'll write.'

'Of course.'

But his smile and his voice seemed not altogether to include her, and she said 'A penny for your thoughts.'

'I was just wondering,' he said, 'where it would be nice to live. Do you like Norfolk? I love the coast of Norfolk. Or Yorkshire? It's just an idea,' he added, turning to her with a bright vague smile.

Just an idea: he was not really questioning her. They were not mad, she repeated inwardly, not sentimental, infantile, romantic. She had come out of the maze in which she had for so long wandered, following love's objects and experiences along blind alleys and bogus turnings. As for him, who had labelled himself an accident in time, release from time's grave had been accomplished. They stood together in a green open country.

Louis was waiting on the shore to greet them; and, leaving him in Louis's hands, she ran on wings across the sand, up the rock terrace between towering bushes of hibiscus. Pausing a moment half-way up to get her breath, she watched a humming bird – incredible, flashing, whirring emerald artefact, not out of nature, pendant against a swag of blossom and intently probing, two inches from her nose.

Princess came drifting down, beautiful in a magenta bodice and full blue and purple skirt, carrying the lamps to the bungalow a little earlier than usual. This time her smile was radiant.

'You look wonderful, Princess – all in your best.'

'Yes Mistress, yes I wait upon the partee. Maybe we make you nice one lei tomorrow for your journee. Maybe I bring my babee to bid au revoir.'

'Yes, do Princess, I'd like to see her.'

'I think maybe you like take her back wid you to England.'

'I think not, Princess. England is cold, not always sun. She would get sick.'

'But you plenty shawls, you keep her warm.'

'Don't you want her yourself, Princess?'

'Not too much wan'. I will have all babies I wan', too many.' She looked dissatisfied. 'Why not you have babies?'

'Maybe I will.'

'Maybe you will.' With a yell of laughter, she set down

a lamp, clumsily plucked a white hibiscus flower, offered it, then changed her mind and stuck it behind her ear.

'Very nice. You are a pretty girl, Princess.'

'Yes, yes!' She began to rock and howl. 'But you more pretty, you the belle!' Her eye fell speculatively on the visitor's one ring, a pink topaz, once her grandmother's. It seemed best to wave and hurry on, pursued by laughter, amid whose paroxysms Princess sent forth a last, plaintive, ringing cry:

'And you smile plen'y to me. When I cheeky you not say I bad. When you go my tears fall down.'

Kit and Trevor, dressed to kill, arrive to escort her to the Cunninghams' farewell party. She wears her best frock – white chiffon faintly patterned with roses and green leaves – to do honour to her hosts. They are among the first to arrive; and find the Captain sitting by himself at the far end of the verandah, mixing cocktails and dispensing them with concentration: also with an air that seems to be saying: Keep your distance. Between puffy lids and cheeks the colour of plums his eyes have almost disappeared. Miss Stay, in orange taffeta, springs out with Ellie from the bedroom and stands to attention behind his chair. Ellie, tightly moulded into her navy hostess gown, is at her most vivacious, trips from guest to guest, now and then tossing a remark or a look in his direction, but not approaching him. Ten o'clock. Two hours to go. Meanwhile a fragment, a facsimile of life among beings of another order must go on, with the absent loved one giving the evening, at one remove, its inexpressible significance. She is two persons, one a smooth surface, one fathomless in depth, each separate from the other.

The Lancashire couple have arrived; also Jackie with the nurses and their escorts. Young Mr de Pas enters with a whoop, crying: 'Toot toot!' Perhaps later on he will be persuaded to do his imitations. Someone starts the gramophone. She dances with Kit, then with Trevor: both are in high spirits, thrilled with the prospect of a change, a journey, and looking forward to her company. Young Mr de Pas ignores his surroundings totally, as usual. Staring ahead, his eyes protuberant, fixed as marbles, he proceeds, with pauses for technical, complicated footwork, round and round the floor with Jackie. His brittle shoulders and ashen-skinned archaic head rise rigidly above her nestling face of a withered English games mistress. A curious couple. They are excellent dancers, they move together in perfect rhythmic harmony. Strange, very strange. Who, to look at her, would have thought that she could glide so smoothly, silkily? She has a high colour, hard, thin, prominent features, brown untidy hair; her teeth stick out. But she has neat athletic legs, also good eyes – large, directly gazing, very blue beneath straight dark eyebrows. She glances at Anonyma without curiosity, smiles in a friendly way. Not a bad girl, Jackie: she has settled for a life of sorts: dancing eternally with Tony de Pas – perhaps, too, watching over his disastrous health; sleeping with him, presumably?

Madge and Phil have each a plump, oleaginous, jet-haired gentleman in tow, and are dancing cheek to cheek. Ellie has tripped to Mr Bartholomew with a stiff whisky, then sits beside him, holding his hand. But she continues to look anxious; her eyes keep sliding towards the Captain and dwelling on Miss Stay.

The Lancashire couple approach. He bows; Miss Cropper beams. 'Mr Crowther,' she says, 'would quite appreciate the favour of a dance. Just keep on humming,' she adds with a nod of encouragement. 'He'll get the drift of it.'

But he does not, or she cannot; and after a faltering shuffle across the floor they desist by mutual agreement. He has taken a fancy to her and keeps a huge paw on her arm as they withdraw to the end of the verandah. Almost at once, in a rumbling bass monotone, he launches into a narrative of his early life, its trials and tribulations, the drama of his confrontations with his alcoholic father.

'I'd leave my bedroom door open and when I heard him come in I'd shout out: "Hypocrite! Bloody hypocrite! Hadn't ought to live!" – meaning he should hear, you understand. Next morning he'd say, "Tom," he'd say, "whatever did you have for soopper last night?" I'd say, "Noothing partickler." "Didn't you have no nightmare?" "No, not me," I'd say. "I slept a treat all through."' Mr Crowther pauses to shake and heave with laughter. 'Oh, there was woon night I recollect. Cooming back from the Social – roaring droonk he was. Shouting all down our street: "Tom you villian, you bloody villian, I've coom to finish you." But first he goes to the lavatory see, that was at the bottom of the garden. I could hear him shoutin' and carryin' on inside and rattlin' at the door fit to wake the whole neighb'rood. The door had got stoock on the inside see – he thought it was me a-holding it on the outside. Oh, the language! – what he'd do to my anatomy when he got out. Three quarters of an hour before he broke that long-sooffering door down and cooms forth bellowin' like a bull to the arenia. I'd nipped up to bed see, and was shammin' sleep. So oop he cooms. "Didn't you hear your poor old Dad?" he says all mild and plaintive, bendin' over me. "Shoot oop!" I says. "What do you mean disturbing me this time of night?"' Another convulsion of genuine amusement. 'Pore old chap. Next morning he'd coom down bright and cheerful just as if there'd been no carry-on. "Good morrow me lads," he'd say. "Good morrow me little pigeons." That's what he'd call me little broothers, Les and Reg – the twins, pore little blighters, they were a burden on me. I never could leave 'im, see. He used to get playin' with the gas mantle. He'd see faces in the carpet – worse than faces. Soom nights he'd just sit by the fire and cry, "I wish my Mary was alive." "Shoot oop," I'd say, "about your Mary. She's a damn sight better off where she is." That was me moother. Everybody 'ad to laugh. "I want to join 'er," e'd moan out. Well, he got his wish. I don't suppose she fancied seein' 'im turn oop, poor Moother. Funny to think of – he was only forty-four. Fine figure of a man he'd been woonce. But he was a right bastard, pore old Dad.'

Miss Cropper has rejoined them, listens reverently, says severely: 'Pneumonia carried him off. What else could you expect?' and goes on to tell how Mr Crowther, orphaned at fourteen, had kept the house going, cared for his little brothers, started them in life. What a sad, dreadful childhood, what a struggle, what an example: a truly wonderful man. Indeed yes. Close on thirty years together now, after his wife – well, the least said about *her* the better: a privilege, every moment of it. Yes; yes indeed: Miss Cropper and the visitor gaze in womanly sympathy at one another. Mr Crowther relapses into non-communication, wearing a look of dignity and satisfaction. Driven by some mysterious compulsion to unfold his story, he has compassed his objective; he is at peace. Presently, with a glance which she cannot fathom from his sunken, shrewd old eyes, he says brusquely:

'You put me in mind of a lass I used to know.' The glance dwells on, transfixes her for a long naked moment.

'That's right,' says Miss Cropper, in matter-of-fact corroboration. 'He had a daughter.'

He drops a heavy paw on his companion's shoulder. 'Coom on then, lass.' Once more they take the floor, revolving together without strict attention to the time. Devotion, thinks the visitor: courage, pride, simplicity; above all humour, no self-pity. Remembering his life, he'd had to laugh.

She decides to join Mr Bartholomew, who sits alone,

bottle beside him, glass in hand.

'Mr Bartholomew!'

He does not respond. How blind, how deaf, is he? She takes the chair beside him; and after a while his black spectacles swivel on her and he says:

'Admired Miranda.'

'Thank you. You haven't ever called me that before.' She feels encouraged. 'Are you fairly happy?'

'No. What a foolish question.'

'Can I do anything for you?'

'No, you cannot. Unless – ' He picks up and shakes the bottle, which emits a reassuring splash. 'Perhaps you will join me?' She refuses with warm thanks. He murmurs: 'A nous autres vieux, c'est la seule consolation qui nous reste.'

'I am going away tomorrow, Mr Bartholomew. Back to England.'

No reply. The gramophone record – a deafening fox-trot – skids to a halt, and in the comparative ensuing silence he remarks:

'That is an abominable cacophony. It lacerates my ear drums.'

'It is trying. You prefer – a more classical type of music?'

'Yes. Are you a musician?'

'Not much of one. I play the piano a little.'

'You have not offered to play to me. No matter. Poor Clementina's instrument is most inferior – in a shocking state. What a cruel deprivation. Chopin – Chopin is my passion. And there are certain French songs . . .' His voice shakes, fades. Mastering emotion, he declares: 'Daisy is passionately fond of music.'

She says lightly, hoping to cheer him up: 'I shall miss all that poetry next door to me. Sometimes, not often of course, I think I could have capped you.'

After a pause he says with querulous venom: 'So you

have been mocking a defenceless old man. Spying on his harmless recreations. Listening at the keyhole. Intruding on his privacy.'

'Never!' she protests, appalled. 'Never! I never mocked. I never listened at the keyhole.' Indignation mounts. 'How can you say such things? You make me angry. You kept me awake. You've been a frightful nuisance, if you want to know. I never complained.'

He seems delighted, breaks into eldritch chuckles. 'Well, well! To think a cultivated young woman was my audience! You should have knocked: who knows? I might have let you in. What then, eh? "Enter Madam. Have no fear, I will respect your virtue. Pray, what can I do for you?" "Sir, I have come to *cap* you." Oh, what a night we would have made of it! *Capping* and *swapping* . . . that's a vulgar word now! It reminds me: I had a friend once, in my salad days. We used to frequent low haunts together, as well as certain private houses where he was enthusiastically received. He had a gift, you see . . .' Again his cracked voice fades. He broods for a moment. 'Frankie his name was, a most amusing and disreputable character. Jewish. A brilliant musician; but he chose to dissipate his talents. He was a *diseur*, an entertainer. Who can resist an entertainer? He could improvise . . . transpose into any key. Ah, magical gift! – his own compositions. They had a flavour which appealed to me; a wit – decadent, ambiguous . . . There was one in particular – how did it go? – it comes back to me whenever Daisy and I watch certain couples through our telescope. You didn't know we had a telescope? Ask Daisy. Now let me see . . . how did it go?'

He starts to emit a toneless thread of sound.

> *By the seashore, perambulating,*
> *We swapped our heartless, witless hearts:*

'A drawing room ballad – with a difference,' he explains. 'Let me see . . .'

> *Was it loving? or was it hating?*
> *Was it a matter of fits and starts?*

'Nostalgic, melancholy, you see. The rest escapes me: it developed a soupçon of salacity, unsuitable for your maiden ears. Catchy, subtle tune to match: it has continued to haunt my imagination *By the seashore, perambulating . . .*'

'What became of Frankie?'

'He came to grief. He had a weakness – ' Mr Bartholomew pauses to refill his glass – 'for appetising boys.'

'I see. Poor Frankie.' It is time to bid farewell. 'Goodbye, Mr Bartholomew. You will be up and away with Daisy when I leave tomorrow morning. Give my love to Daisy.'

'I may and I may not. Where is Miss Stay? Out of respect for our good host and hostess I agreed to attend this preposterous function. But enough is enough. I am more than ready to depart. I shall be obliged if you will seek out Miss Stay and tell her so.'

'I will. Goodbye, Mr Bartholomew. Don't forget me.'

'I shall have forgotten you by – let me see – the day after tomorrow.'

Before she reaches the Captain's corner, Miss Stay has started briskly to advance, crying in rapturous greeting: 'Ah! Our ray of sunshine! What an extra special glow tonight. You and our dear permanent lodger will have been having a most interesting chat.'

'Very interesting. I'm afraid he hates me.'

'Oh, hush dear! Perish the thought! Try to surround him with lashings of light and love. He is in need of it.'

'Well . . . I'll try. But I don't find him lovable.'

'There you have a point, I grant you. He is *not* running over with the milk of human kindness. All the more reason to dispense it in full measure. To counteract, you know, what he is open to.'

'What is he open to?'

'Dark forces,' declares Miss Stay, winking one eye with the unintentional effect of imparting some lewd confidence. 'I fancy our friend went far at one time into – shall we say the Mysteries? without asking for protection. A recipe for mortal danger.'

'You mean he's a magician? I see he might be – a wicked old magician. Perhaps Daisy is his familiar.'

'Oh, hush hush *hush* dear! A joke is a joke, but . . .' Miss Stay places a leathery hand over the lips of the visitor who takes it and lays it against her cheek, saying:

'You are an angel. I hope he's never horrid to you.'

'Bless you!' Miss Stay is startled, touched. 'Me an angel? This old scarecrow? Enough to make the angels weep, more likely! Oh, I take no notice – the poor wee shivering scared shrimp. Due to go over soon. All unprepared.' With another convulsive wink she adds: 'We must pray . . . Now I must buzz off home with him. Bye bye dearie.'

Ellie, being led out to foxtrot by Trevor, calls out: 'Anemone, have a little chat with Harold, there's a love. He's feeling a bit seedy, it's nothing much.'

'Harold?' She perches on a stool beside his old armchair. He gives her a rapid sketch of a smile; but he is looking far from healthy.

'I hoped you were going to sing tonight.'

He cups his ear, saying: 'Sorry, bit deaf, this infernal din'; and she repeats the words, which now sound singularly vapid.

'Christ no! Not on your effing life. Nobody wants . . .' His voice trails off; it sounds faintly slurred. Could he be drunk?

'Where's Bobby?'

'Taken himself off. Don't blame him. Poor old sod. Poor bleeding bugger.'

The Captain's code of gentlemanliness seems at risk. She wishes in vain for an appropriate comment from Miss Stay to raise the low vibrations. She takes his hand and strokes it: yet another worn unsightly hand in hers, she thinks: this is the saddest – simply an old man's powerless hand.

'Dear Harold, I'm afraid you're not feeling very well.'

'Who, me? I'm fit as a flea, thanks all the same. Felt a bit wonky earlier on. Fact is m'dear went out on the tiles last night – Jackie and her chums – jolly crowd. That's strictly on the q.t. Madam – m'lady wife's annoyed. Don't blame her. Not as young as I was, hach! hach! No fool like an old fool, eh? But tophole now. Fit as a flea. Enjoying m'self. Are you?' He looks at her shyly, with affection.

'Oh yes. It's so sweet of you and Ellie to give this party. You take so much trouble for your guests.'

'Not at all. A pleasure. She enjoys it.' He adds gruffly: 'Fact is, the girl gets lonely. We all do now and then out here, y'know. She's only a girl.'

'I shall miss you both. She's been so good to me, you both have. I shall never forget the kindness. I don't know – I simply can't think – what I'd have done without you.' She swallows a lump in her throat.

'Don't mention it. We'll miss you too. Hope you'll come back another year. Not often we . . .' His face works; he reaches for a glass, but there is none beside him. He glares at the dancers, growls ferociously: 'Where is she? Can't spot her. Who's she dancing with?'

'Who? Ellie?'

'No, no,' he says irritably. 'That Madge.'

Next moment the dark nurse Madge, the one with the sulky sensual mouth, comes slouching up, stands before them in a characteristic stance – shoulders hunched, head poking forward, hips swaying languorously. She runs a semi-professional eye over the Captain and enquires in a sing song nasal drawl:

'And how's his Nibs tonight? None the worse, eh?' With a bold glance at the visitor she adds: 'He deserves a good spanking, he's a naughty boy. Giving us all a fright.' Her manner combines nonchalance with a somehow proprietary conniving air.

'Take a pew, take a pew,' shouts the now animated Captain. 'Fit as a fiddle. Take a pew.'

Casting to the winds all semblance of old-world British decency, let alone courtesy, he contrives, by sheer determination, to oust his wife's best friend from her seat beside him and to install the intruder in her place.

Ellie comes by, mutters 'Anemone', seizes her by the arm and draws her away from the verandah into her bedroom. It is a plain sparsely furnished room. Austere twin beds in shadow suggest a long habit of counter-erotic nuptial intimacy. Ellie flings herself down on one of them and motions the visitor to sit beside her.

'What do you think of her?' she says abruptly. 'That Madge creature.'

'She's horrible.'

'Isn't she? She's *nasty*.'

'If I were you I wouldn't have her in the house.'

'Shall I kick her out?' She jumps to her feet, draws herself up to all of five feet two, assuming a haughty and contemptuous expression. 'Oh, Nemone, I'm worried. I haven't seen you all day. I know, I know: Staycie said Johnny wanted to take you on a fishing trip, I'm so glad, did you have a happy day?'

'Very happy.' She feels guilt-stricken. 'What's the matter, darling? Is Harold – '

'I wish I knew. What *is* the matter? How do you think he looks?'

'Well . . . Rather tired.'

'He's not himself at all.' She wanders to the dressing table, touching objects aimlessly. 'If you want to know, he didn't come home all night. He's done it before. I wasn't too worried, though I get fed up of course . . . But Jackie and Tony breezed in this morning before I was dressed. I'd guessed he'd been with them on an all-night binge: disgusting, isn't it? I don't know where they go. Still, Jackie's not a bad sort . . . and men do need a bit of an outlet now and then. Anyway, what do you suppose she said? I wasn't to worry but he'd had a little *turn*.'

'What did she mean?'

'It *wasn't* a stroke, she said – but a sort of come-over . . . After all, she is a nurse. They'd put him to bed at Tony's – Tony's extremely eccentric but he's kind; and they'd taken turns to sit up with him, including that Madge you bet – and his pulse and everything was normal and he'd had a light breakfast and wanted to get back as soon as possible. Worrying about *me*, she said: much more likely Bobby. Anyway, later in the morning Tony drove him back. He looked mouldy and he didn't want to talk – but that's quite usual. He's slept most of the day. He hasn't touched a drop. But I keep thinking his speech is a bit affected. Did you notice?'

She said falsely that she had noticed nothing; adding: 'Surely he always talks like that? – a little sort of slurred and clipped? I took it to be traditional British military speech. An army wife like you would be too used to it to notice.'

'I hope you're right,' exclaims Ellie, more cheerfully. 'I expect you are. It's true. I don't always listen to poor old Harold. Nor he to me, for that matter.'

'Why don't you get the doctor to give him a check-up? I suppose there is a doctor on the island?'

'I might. It would mean going over to Port of Spain.

There is a doctor here of sorts, but he's always drunk.' She powdered her nose, put on more lipstick, touched up her hair. 'Staycie's given him healing, she says I needn't get alarmed. Still, I don't want this party to go on too late. Oh, why aren't you staying and that *bitch* leaving tomorrow? What can she see in him? Of course, she's man-mad. Do you know what I heard her say in that awful gluey voice of hers? She always *goes for the older man!* Flattery, you see – he laps it up. He can't bear for her to leave his side. Seeing she's a nurse and him in a dicky state I don't quite dare to see her off. Oh, aren't men idiots, isn't sex the limit?' She takes a framed photograph from the dressing table and hands it to her friend. 'That's Mummy. Taken when I was about six.'

The picture shows a youngish woman with a pleasant smile, an Edwardian coiffure, a lace blouse with a high boned collar. Her little daughter, in dainty frills, with corkscrew curls, leans against her shoulder. 'That's the last,' says Ellie, 'she ever had taken – the last studio portrait. Harold took some snaps in the garden not long before the end, but I can't put them out, they make me feel so sad.'

'What a sweet face. And you – you've hardly changed.'

'How can you say so? But I was a pretty girl. Harold used to call me his little bit of Dresden china.' She looks searchingly at the photograph before replacing it. 'She's gone a long way on now, I expect, but we're never really out of touch. She'd know if I was in for trouble before I knew it myself.' She broods, her round blue innocent eyes dilated. 'If you remember, it was in the cards.'

'Trouble?'

She nods. 'But I *must not* harbour morbid thoughts. I'll just say this out once – to you, then throw it off. *If* Harold's going to – go downhill bit by bit – get helpless, get – you know, silly, turn against me – they do, you know – I don't see how I could bear it.' She collapses again on the bed and bursts into tears on her friend's shoulder, sobbing out: 'I get to feel so lonely.'

From the bottom of her heart, Anemone dispenses reassurance, sympathy; and presently she brightens, bathes her eyes, apologises, agrees that she's lucky to have Staycie to support her; and then there's Johnny, how lucky to have a wonderful man like him for a friend; says that now she's got a real friend in England she'll save up for a trip one of these fine days and pay her a nice long visit.

'Yes, you must promise,' says Anemone.

'And you will write, won't you? I feel in my bones a lovely surprise is going to come along for you when you get back. Mind you let me know.'

'Of course I will.' She is seized by an impulse to laugh aloud.

'Mr Right at last! – that's what I hope.' Ellie becomes thoughtful. 'You know, I'm afraid Johnny's going to miss you.'

'Oh, I don't think he will . . .'

'Yes, you've made a difference to him. I can't quite put my finger on it, but you have. It's as if he had a candle lit inside him. I've noticed him looking at you – and teasing you.'

'He teases you too.'

'Yes, but not in the same way. I've almost felt jealous of you once or twice but I know it's silly. Anyway, I'm too fond of you both to be jealous. I'm just glad when I see him in good spirits. Taking you on this trip today shows how much he likes you. Not that he ever shows his feelings . . . But I wish he was here tonight. I would have thought your last night . . . It's not the same without him. He lends such distinction . . . What *can* be happening?'

The sounds of shrieks of hilarity interrupts this tête à tête. What a mercy! – just in the nick of time. The temptation to confide in Ellie has become almost overwhelming.

They hurry back to the verandah, to be greeted by a bizarre spectacle. Young Mr de Pas has somehow got hold of a spare mosquito net and has donned it like a hieratic vestment. Its circular frame balanced on his head, its ample draperies floating and billowing round him, he performs a stately dance to the tune of a tango. Up and down the room he sweeps, a towering ghost, snapping his fingers, stamping, swirling with a flourish to a standstill. Seeing Ellie, he glides forward, parts his drapes in silence, with a dramatic gesture draws her within their folds and dances on. Now begins a double act, hysterically comic: they swoop and sway as if in a crazy bridal tangle. Mr Crowther roars and beats his thighs; even the Captain is wiping his eyes, in fits. The nurses wear a detached expression, as if deploring infantile behaviour. Jackie tolerantly smiles. Finally, Ellie kicks a roguish heel up and emerges, flushed, dishevelled, gasping; runs to the Captain, from whose side Madge slouchingly withdraws.

Oh, what fun, what fun! What a scream is Tony. Flinging off his lendings, he advances to bow low before the Captain, solemnly kisses Ellie's hand; together they face their guests, acknowledging applause. He ought to be on the Halls. Never as long as they live . . . and Ellie! if ever there was a dark horse . . . What a gorgeous climax to a splendid evening. For now they must depart. Miss Stay, having dealt with her Ancient, has reappeared to hustle them away. With hearty thanks they all drift off. Miss Stay will sleep down here in the spare room, just to be on call in case.

Ellie is safe; nothing threatens her. The crown of the evening's fun has lighted on her head. Soon she will get busy, tidying up; she will whistle for Bobby, call goodnight to Joey in the eaves. But now, successful hostess, she stands beside her Captain.

Midnight. She is alone, negotiating the rock path towards the shore, threading the myriad crepitations, sibilant whispers, the wires and strings that pluck the dark. Balm, spices, honeyed fragrance, showers of stars pour over her as from an invisible vast cornucopia; a soft flurry of fireflies surrounds her head. Something brushes past her with a snuffle and a click of claws: Bobby returning home from some nocturnal occasion of his own: *By the seashore, perambulating* . . .

No light illumines her destination. Yes! – all at once a blaze in the sea-grape tree. She runs.

Johnny is standing underneath the tree, leaning against its trunk, dappled from head to foot with disks of leaf reflection, so that he looks half dematerialized in light and shadow. He has a cape slung over his shoulders: the blue cloak of Mrs Jardine. When, breath-stopped, incredulous again, she reaches him he wraps it round them both. The breeze is cool.

'Punctual,' he murmurs.

'I was afraid I'd never get away. Suddenly it worked like magic.'

'Well now,' he says softly. 'We must say goodbye. Have a pleasant journey. Keep safe. Be a good girl. Write to me.' His tone is practical.

'Of course. I'm not absolutely sure I know your surname.'

'The name is Gourlay. John David Gourlay.'

'A nice name.'

He laughs a little. 'I'm glad you like it. It's going to be yours one day.'

She catches her breath. 'Oh! . . . How incredible. And what about *my* name, my address? Don't you want it?'

'Yes. But you haven't got one, have you?' Taken aback, she looks up at him – and he laughs again. 'Not a steady one – or so you said.'

'Did I? It's true I'm not sure where . . . My cottage is

let, and . . . I dare say I'll go home – for a bit; and then . . . I can't seem to think. But I will.'

'I wouldn't like important documents, addressed to Anonyma, to go astray. You write to me, I'll answer. I might even send a cable.'

Her head spins, she holds him closer. 'Johnny, I'm not dreaming, am I?

He shakes his head, heaves a big sigh, says oddly: 'It's the grand passion.'

'About this baby: in another month I suppose I'll know for sure. I'm to let you know at once?'

'Of course.'

'Supposing – supposing I've made a mistake. What then?'

'*Oh*! you said you were sure,' he exclaims, mock re-proachful. 'The thing is, can I trust you? How can I be certain? You might try to palm it off on – someone else.' He holds her away from him, shakes her. 'Look at me. Swear.'

'I swear.' Their eyes meet in a drowning gaze, seeing far back behind the eyes to the essential imprint. But surely he has faithless eyes? . . . And what can hers be telling him? 'How could you even imagine such a thing? How could you?'

All he says is: 'If you did I'd come and kill you'; and wraps her up again.

'How can *I* be certain? Are you *promising* to come?'

'I promise.'

'When?'

'Oh . . . before long. As soon as I can. I must get just a bit better. Get absolutely fit.'

'Darling, don't wait for that. I'll make you absolutely better when you come.'

'Yes,' he says, rather vaguely now. And then, with a mixture of mock-severity and ruefulness: 'I'm a married man, you know. I must get a divorce – or she must. You must be protected.'

'Protected?'

'Naturally I intend to see you are not *affichée* in the case.'

'I wouldn't care.'

'I care,' he says, genuinely severe.

How strange such words, such concepts sound tonight, on a West Indian shore.

' "Protected", "*Affichée*" . . . Those are Sibyl words.' She touches the collar of his cape. 'Her cloak.'

'Yes, that's all right,' he says, as if dismissing an irrelevance. 'Listen. I want you to take this.' He pulls from the pocket of his slacks the gold medallion that he often wears: a finely engraved circular locket with a central diamond. 'Bend your head.' Carefully he slips it over her head on its gold Victorian chain. 'Don't look so doubtful. It was my mother's and before that my grandmother's. I was to give it to the girl I meant to marry. I wore it all through the war as a mascot. Then I crashed; and you know what happened. So I didn't give it to that girl I've mentioned, though I'd meant to. The last time she came to see me, when I told her – I told her a clean break was best, there was this little heirloom: she wouldn't take it, she was quite right. But we made a sort of pact. I was to let her know if something happened to me, if ever I had a life again, or if ever I disappeared, I would somehow let her know. There . . . it opens, but don't open it. There's a screw of paper inside with her name and address on it. It won't bother you, it's only an address, no message or anything of that sort. Just keep it, forget about it till I come for you.'

'And when you come for me?'

'Oh, when I come for you!' – the words ring like a ballad, with a dark undertone – 'I'll cope with everything. I just don't want to take any risks, leave any loose ends, between now and when I depart. I suppose I'm superstitious.'

'I think I won't wear it much until you come; but I'll look after it very very carefully.'

'It's yours.'

'It's precious.' She holds it a moment and puts it to her lips. 'Here's my ring for you, in exchange: *my* heirloom thing, my grandmother's pink topaz.' She draws it off and gives it to him; but it is too small for his little finger, and he returns it to her saying:

'No, no, let's wait to give each other rings. Things have a way of disappearing here.'

'What will you do about Louis?'

'Ah, Louis . . . I'll have to think. Why shouldn't he come too?'

'Why not? *Johnny*!' Is it his heart, or hers beating so turbulently? 'Say it will come true. For the rest of our lives.'

'For the rest of our lives?' He makes it almost a question, then says, after a pause: 'We can but try.' A strange thing to say: as if he were facing a mystifying problem; some sort of grave operation whose outcome is uncertain. Yet his face remains serene; as if, on some other level, the solution is discerned.

'Remember,' she says, 'if it gets to seem too difficult, it wouldn't *really* matter. I wouldn't feel let down. It couldn't make any difference. You will always be my love. You have changed my life.'

'And you mine.'

'If I don't go now, I never shall.' Silent, he throws his head back so that the light plays fully on it; his smile dazzles her. 'Remember my real name, won't you?'

One eyebrow shoots up, he nods, murmurs teasingly, drawing out the syllables: 'A – non – y – ma.'

She walks away, telling herself: I won't turn back, I

mustn't look back. But presently her plodding feet in the soft sand are halted. She turns. He is still underneath the tree, he has not moved. Now he looks infinitely far away: more than spatial distance seems to separate her from him. It has again become a question of Time's bewildering telescopic lens. With that cloak flung back, with his romantic head inclined, the shadows of sea-grape clusters like dark curls falling to his shoulders, with his patterned torso and unnaturally long legs lightly crossed, he has become an archetypal Renaissance figure: Portrait of an Unknown Youth in a bower of leaves.

Shortly after dawn comes the hour of her departure: too early, thank heaven, for a large and demonstrative farewell gathering. Princess carrying baby No Name, Carlotta, Adelina, Winkliff and Deshabille come in as she drinks her coffee bearing a magnificent lei of jasmine and hibiscus. They hang it round her neck. She hugs them, tips them lavishly. All are in tears, except for No Name who, received into her godmother's arms for an official blessing, accepts a kiss impassively. She is plump as a pigeon with a ripe blackberry lustre on her skin, altogether delicious, dressed – to impress – in layer after layer of pink and blue flannel and sprigged cotton, with red coral earrings and a necklace of black and scarlet beads, like ladybirds. She nestles contentedly and makes a dive at once for the visitor's breast: a happy omen noted with approval by Princess and the rest of her cortège. 'She wan' not leave you,' murmurs her mother with a final spurt of hope. The visitor sticks a sprig of jasmine behind one neat close-fitting ear and yields her back, experiencing a pang and promising not to forget to send a bracelet. After pocketing their tips, the boys stand stiffly at attention. They have rehearsed the Boy Scout salute, and now render it in silence and solemnity.

Miss Stay appears, and shoos them all away. Manageress and visitor are alone together, as they were in this very room, in another lifetime, three weeks ago.

'A sight for sore eyes, a mortal treat!' exclaims Miss Stay. 'The springing tread, the sparkling eyes . . . those sad sad anxious furrows all smoothed out.' Gently she touches the visitor's forehead between the eyes, smoothes it with outward strokes above the eyebrows, over the temples. 'At your age to look so careworn! It was a mortal shame. Your dear mother will rejoice to see her daughter restored to glorious health.'

'I suppose she will.' But, thinks her mother's daughter, a distrustful eye will be run over me . . . 'You have all been so kind to me, especially you, dear darling Miss Stay. I don't know how to thank you. I don't think I'd have been alive now if I hadn't landed up here.'

'Ah, it was meant – no doubt of that. Though what,' continues Miss Stay pursuing a maternal image of her own devising, 'she will say to the crowning glory is beyond me to conceive. How does the poet put it? *What's become of all the gold?* – speaking if I recollect aright of dear dead females he had fancied.'

'My hair – doesn't it look awful? Never mind. I've got your egg and brandy recipe, it will soon recover. I expect there's a first-class hairdresser on our super luxury liner.'

'Pure auburn deepening to chestnut,' broods Miss Stay. 'Quite an original combination. Ah me! – to them that have . . .' And now, from the depths of those dark hypnotic pits, her eyes, she looks fully at the visitor. 'It's been a great pleasure to have you with us, Miss Anemone. Such an addition. This establishment is a wee thought on the primitive side I grant you, but we provide *something*, I venture to believe. Perhaps a healing atmosphere. And the girls are loving girls – good and naughty, all are loving girls. Ellie will miss you sorely, Miss Anemone. A faithful

156

female friend is what she lacks.'

'I shall miss her too. I've promised to keep in touch with her. But she can't lack a faithful female friend as long as she's got you.'

'Oh, she's got her old Staycie, never fear. But Staycie may be leaving before long.'

'Leaving? Oh dear, that would be a blow to her; and to Harold; and – ' She cannot pronounce the name of Johnny, and adds lamely: 'and to Mr Bartholomew. What would he do without you?'

'Ah, don't worry, I shall wait to see him over. Any time now – any time.'

'You mean – he won't live much longer?'

'I mean that. His course is nearly run. Now and again he has a despondent turn. I tell him his contribution is not to be despised: he has made his own contribution. Sensitive as you are, dear, you will grasp my meaning.'

'Well . . . He certainly makes a powerful impact.'

'Speaking as one with a lifetime of hotel management behind her, I deplore the inconvenience. But there's love among the cinders there – that's the thing to cling to.'

'You mean his feeling for Daisy?'

'I knew you would catch on. I grant you in this instance love has run amok, but who are we to judge? It's a beginning. Better to have loved and – well – than never to have loved at all. Tempered by wisdom it will stand him in good stead his next time down. I see him as a high-up in the bloodstock line; or as a grand worker, maybe, for poor, goaded, belaboured, patient animals in the evening of their days. Remember him in your prayers, dear. He is in need of them.'

'I don't pray, I'm afraid, I don't know how. Perhaps I will learn some day.'

'You will. You will.'

'But I'd do anything for you, Miss Stay.'

Suddenly Miss Stay abandons her contortions, facial

and verbal, and says quietly: 'Do you mean that?'

'Yes – I do.'

'Then care for my lamb, should occasion offer.' She gestures in the direction of the bungalow. 'Should she ever come to England your paths might cross again. She might need help, and you could give it.'

'Of course. I'd always help her if I could. But I do hope – you sound rather – I do hope she's not likely to need anybody's help. How is the Captain this morning?'

'Not stirring when I left – nor Ellie either. Oh, the Captain's not about to kick the bucket by a long chalk. He has the constitution of an ox.' Pensively she adds: 'And a virile chap to boot.'

'They are the dearest people. They have both been so good to me. Everybody has.'

'The truth is you're a perfect little catalyst, as I've said before,' exclaims Miss Stay.

'I wonder what you mean. That I cause changes in people? – in their lives? How can I? How do I do it?'

'Oh, not by meddling! – not by wiles and guileful-nesses – quite the contrary. Sometimes it takes an inno-cent, Mistress Anemone, to be a catalyst. I fancy it is written in your destiny. *There's* the mystery.'

Casting a rapid backward glance over her troubled wavering life history, the visitor thinks, with consterna-tion, that this judgment might contain a truth.

'A stranger bringing changes, that is what showed up – or seemed to.' Miss Stay's tone is dreamy. She adds with a delicate hint of triumph: 'And thus it has turned out. Now wouldn't you agree?'

'Certainly *my* life has changed.' She blushes.

'Mysterious are His ways,' acknowledges Miss Stay. 'Deep called to deep.'

'You said – there would be a miracle,' stammers the other, feeling the blush take over uncontrollably. 'I wonder, did you mean – what's happened? You know, don't you, what has happened?' Miss Stay is silent. 'Do you think he will be – what you hoped, expected – saved?' Lamely she concludes: 'What he said he didn't want to be.'

Miss Stay now appears to be returning from a far journey. After a pregnant pause she sighs, then mutters: 'Yes. Yes. All is well.'

What can she be getting at? The visitor superstitiously fingers the medallion hidden beneath her blouse. Tension grows in the empty dining room: it is as if a long withdrawing wave of air were being sucked out, out.

At this moment Winkliff appears from the verandah with a basketful of fresh-picked flowers. Miss Stay receives it from him and begins to make up mixed bouquets and plunge them into the little Victorian glass table vases. She is fully awake now, voluble, vivacious, twitching.

'Ah, it was a mortal shame. Poor blessed woman, how I pitied her. She went into deep waters – deep deep waters, they closed over her. And ever since? . . . Oh, now and then I have been tempted to despair.' Her floral task accomplished, she stands rocking on her heels, her head flung back. 'Take you and I dear, place us side by side, even our guardian angels might conclude one of us cannot be a woman. But I am one!' Her arms fly up, she strikes her breast. 'I love the man. I would have died for him. Well, now I need not!' Wiping her eyes, she chuckles – a youthful cheerful sound, before which the visitor cannot but feel abashed. 'You are a sly puss, Mistress Nemone! However, the wind bloweth where it . . . ' Again she chuckles, vehemently nods. 'Who knows? Maybe *she* had a hand in it. Who is to say? It would be like her, eh? Should she pull him over? Should she let him go? Destroy him? Save him? I take it she was ever one to take her opportunities regardless – '

'She was ruthless,' admits the candidate.

'And do herself some good to boot,' continues Miss

Stay, equally regardless. '*You* were her opportunity, heaven sent – in a manner of speaking heaven sent.'

'I think she really wished me well; she was always fond of me,' protests the candidate, trying for strict fairness with a dash of pity. 'And she must have loved him very much.'

'No doubt of that. Ah well! he's safe now: she can't pull him over. The world tastes sweet to him again – the world, the flesh – hmm hmm . . .'

'We love each other,' cries the departing visitor. 'It's more than – I adore him. It's nothing to do with her, with anybody else. You must believe it!'

'I do.' Miss Stay is soothing. 'No, no, she's gone. Bless her, that's one of us saved, that's one thing certain.'

'You said once . . . He told me you said you didn't expect him to make old bones.'

'Did I say that? That's just old woman talk, you must know that: just cackling old nurse's talk. Don't give it another thought.'

A car has been climbing the steep drive from the plantation road. It stops. Next moment Kit and Trevor have appeared, with shining morning faces, with immaculate new shirts, one rose, one duck egg blue, bow ties, cream shantung suits.

'God bless you,' says Miss Stay. 'God keep you.'

They embrace.

'Take care of him,' whispers the visitor.

While the luggage is being stowed she runs to the verandah for one last look across the flowering terraces down to the bay, ablaze with morning sun. No boat. No figure moving. No sign of that white ever-wheeling bird. Dissolved in light, the hut, the sea-grape tree have disappeared.

POSTSCRIPT

My last novel was *A Sea-Grape Tree*, published in 1976, a sequel
to *The Ballad and the Source*. I have, in my mind, a third novel in
the sequence, which will now never be written, which draws
together the threads of the first two books. But first, for those
readers who may wish to be reminded of these novels, I shall
attempt to reintroduce, briefly, some of the characters.

The Ballad and the Source spans the years of the Great War. The
story unfolds through the eyes of Rebecca Landon, a ten-year-
old, who lives with her family in the quiet of the English
countryside. Through Rebecca we meet the scandalous Jardine
family, who have returned to the country and live near the
Landons: the enigmatic Sibyl, and her grandchildren Malcolm
and Maisie (who is to be become, for Rebecca, 'the first woman
friend I ever had'). It is, however, Mrs Jardine who is the
central character of the novel, a woman with a passionate,
stormy past, who is to haunt Rebecca throughout her life.

Sixteen years later we encounter Rebecca again in *A Sea-
Grape Tree*. Deserted by her un-named, married lover, she
travels alone to a magical island in the Tropics. Here she meets
Johnny who tells Rebecca that Sibyl Jardine is buried on the
island. The other residents include Miss Stay, presiding genius
and advanced psychic; Captain and Mrs (Ellie) Cunningham;
Tony de Pas, the local plantation owner; Kit and Trevor,
artistic lovers; and the once dashing Johnny, Mrs Jardine's last
adored protégé, paralysed from the waist down in the First
World War, his servant Louis, and his wife and nurse Jackie.
Rebecca (or 'Anonyma' as she is known on the mysterious Isle)
has a passionate affair with the reclusive Johnny, and as a token
of his trust he gives her a medallion: inside is the address of the
girl, Sylvia, he was to have married before his accident. Rebecca
leaves the Isle with two promises: the first is to Miss Stay, to

161

care for her 'lamb', Ellie Cunningham, 'should occasion offer'; the second to Johnny, to pass the medallion to his former love should anything happen to him. But what echoes in her mind long after she leaves is neither of these two charges – it is the conversation she has had with the vibrant spirit of Mrs Jardine, who is still haunting the island and all its inhabitants. Her sinister shadow is finally lifted.

A Sea-Grape Tree is generally considered an unsatisfactory work. It would ill become me to argue for it; but perhaps I might just venture to say that Anonyma's conversation with Sibyl Jardine was intended to be a telepathic one. Telepathy between the incarnate and the discarnate is much less uncommon than is generally supposed. Sibyl is made to speak as she spoke on earth, as in *The Ballad and the Source*, in a somewhat didactic or mandarin style; but I see the experiment was rash and courted irritation, head-shaking, even mockery from a few critics ever willing and never afraid to wound. The action takes place on the brink, as it were, of another dimension, part poetic, out of time, part realistic: a kind of fabled or Prospero-type isle, where misfits, exiles in the world's terms, shipwrecked people, are washed up, find shelter, healing, loving kindness; even the dream of love accepted and fulfilled. In her generous and beautiful introduction to this edition, Janet Watts writes that the book requires a sequel. I did intend one. For the last time, I imagined, my 'daimon' descended, as of old, and drew back the curtain, showing me in one flash the entire landscape with figures, static, waiting to be animated, woven into an organic pattern. I saw it all; I knew it could be done, but the prospect daunted me, the energy required seemed altogether lacking. I have never in my life made a synopsis or sketched out a plot beforehand, but I do quite often think about this novel, seeing particular vignettes with clarity. This postscript gives a rough idea of this book that I shall never write.

The world of myth and magic is left behind for good; Anonyma resumes her name, Rebecca, and returns to 'ordinary life'. She goes back to the flat which she had shared part-time with her lover. She discovers the extraordinary reason why he failed to keep his date when she embarked for that tropic isle. The reason is quite clear in my mind, but I wish to keep it a secret. She breaks with him, and he disappears. Johnny writes that he will be with her exactly a year from now, but he does not come. It is now 1939. She hears, probably through Kit and Trevor, with whom she has kept in touch, the appalling news. Tragedy has struck the island. Tony de Pas has been murdered, found shot dead in his car. By whom? It is not known, but he had many enemies. Jackie, who loved him, is distraught. Johnny moves back to his own house on the hill, which he had left whilst having his affair with Rebecca, feeling that he cannot desert Jackie until she has recovered. After all, he married her, he says, and he is an honourable man. He says he will come as soon as he possibly can.

After that, months of silence from the Isle; and now it is September 1939. Rebecca has a compulsion to go in search of Maisie, and she finds her, running, perhaps, a maternity clinic in the East End, and it is from Maisie she hears the truth. Remember that Maisie was there when Sibyl Jardine died, and had made friends with all the community on the island. Johnny died in Louis' arms, without warning, of a heart attack. I don't see any of this clearly, but what is vivid is that Rebecca gets into her car and goes to somewhere in the West Country to return the medallion to Sylvia as she has promised. From the lane she watches Sylvia in the rather large garden of her thatched cottage, picking blackcurrants. I see exactly what Sylvia looks like – rather faded and untidy, nice face, wearing slacks. In the end Rebecca simply slips the medallion through the flap of the letter-box and drives away. On the journey back it suddenly strikes her: 'But he knew he would never come back. He must have known even when he gave me the medallion.' War breaks out. She and Maisie have re-established their old intimacy and she agrees to take Tarni, Maisie's daughter, and perhaps one or two other children to her cottage in the country out of reach of the bombs. Tarni's father? Oh, Tarni is the fruit of a casual encounter on a walking tour, perhaps in France. 'I told you', said Maisie, 'I would never marry, but it doesn't mean I preserved my sacred virginity – not by a long chalk.'

Now comes Part II, and I think Rebecca writes it in the first person. This is mainly the story of Ellie Cunningham, whom she runs into by chance on a brief visit to London. Ellie has changed her name to Mrs Macleod, 'Mummy's name', has inherited a large, dreary London house from her only relative, an aunt, and has become an anxious, haggard landlady, keeping up soignée, lady-like appearances. She does fire watching. She takes lodgers, whom she distrusts, and finds 'very common, but you can't be too choosey'. But what has happened to her husband the Captain? 'Oh, he became totally infatuated with that awful nurse.' Told Ellie to clear out. 'It was sex,' says Ellie. Shortly after he had a massive stroke, and that was that. Rebecca recalls her promise to Miss Stay of the Isle, now passed on, to care for her lamb if she ever had occasion, and starts befriending Ellie, though with a sinking, uncharitable heart. Ellie has become more and more of a bore and a chatterbox; she has retained something of her pre-1914 appearance of a pretty woman ('She has much thicker hair than she used to have and the colour seems unreal. Can it be a wig?') She doesn't like dwelling on the past; it is too painful, but comforts herself with pious slogans. Sometimes Rebecca hears her murmuring 'God is kind.' She invites her to her cottage for the weekend, and Ellie and Tarni strike up a close schoolgirl friendship. They gossip together and garden, and wash their hair. Ellie teaches her to cut out and sew. Tarni has inherited much of her great-grandmother Sibyl Jardine's beauty, but *not* her character. She is a splendid girl – candid, stubborn, literal-minded, good as gold. After a couple of gin and tonics at the village pub Ellie bursts into tears, and out come all her woes. She has had hopes: her solicitor, a little younger of course, but not all that much, had obviously fancied her; taken her out to supper, gone home with her, made love to her. But she hadn't seen him since. Once or twice she rang up, and he always made excuses. But she's so lonely. She longs for a man in her life: she's a born homemaker, she says. Surely she has much to offer. 'There must be lots of lonely chappies, widowers retired from service abroad, still active and healthy – a gentleman, of course, it would have to be.' She's heard of a certain highly recommended Marriage Bureau. What does Rebecca think? Rebecca, of course, is only too happy to pay the quite stiff entrance fee. Hopes revived, Ellie has been introduced to a rather attractive, middle-aged bachelor, retired from the Indian Civil Service, so there is much in common.

Time passes – no word from Ellie. The telephone seems out of order, or is never answered. Finally Rebecca rings up the Marriage Bureau. 'I am sorry to tell you, my dear, that Mrs Macleod lied to us about her age. We cannot have *that* sort of thing. It would give us a bad name.' And where is she? They have no idea, she's no longer on their books. Next Rebecca hears that Ellie is in hospital. She goes to visit her, and finds her in a Jerry-built annexe of an evacuated hospital somewhere not too far away. At first she does not recognize her. She's deteriorating rapidly but still hopes that her friend the solicitor will pay her a visit – he has promised to do so. Tarni is very upset, she goes red in the face with angry, choked-back tears, when she hears that Ellie has died. 'She was nicer than, much nicer than –' I waited '– than almost anyone,' says Tarni. She insists on going to the funeral with Rebecca, carrying a huge bunch of flowers. Ellie is buried, by her request, beside 'Mummy', in a pleasant country churchyard. The only other mourner is the solicitor, a smooth-faced, old-young man wearing an old school tie. He has an opaque, cold eye. 'She was my mother's friend,' he says more than once, in case of any misunderstanding about her age and status in his eyes. Rebecca goes back to the hospital to collect poor Ellie's things which have been left to her, and a stout, plain, bespectacled nurse who had been kind to Ellie says 'She wandered sometimes near the end. They do, you know. She would keep on saying "Stay, stay" – something like that. Well, at first I thought she was on about her stays, or else she was wanting more of my attention, but I had plenty of other patients to see to. At the very end, about 3 a.m. one night, she opened her eyes wide, and gave such a smile and said that word again. "Stay", it sounded like.' (Ellie is seeing Miss Stay, Staycie, who has 'come to fetch her over' as she had promised, long ago.)

Most of this is taken straight from life, sad life. I knew the original of Ellie quite well during the War. She left me her only trinket, a little brooch. It has disappeared.

Rosamond Lehmann, London, 1985

VIRAGO MODERN CLASSICS
&
CLASSIC NON-FICTION

The first Virago Modern Classic, *Frost in May* by Antonia White, was published in 1978. It launched a list dedicated to the celebration of women writers and to the rediscovery and reprinting of their works. Its aim was, and is, to demonstrate the existence of a female tradition in fiction, and to broaden the sometimes narrow definition of a 'classic' which has often led to the neglect of interesting novels and short stories. Published with new introductions by some of today's best writers, the books are chosen for many reasons: they may be great works of fiction; they may be wonderful period pieces; they may reveal particular aspects of women's lives; they may be classics of comedy or storytelling.

The companion series, Virago Classic Non-Fiction, includes diaries, letters, literary criticism, and biographies – often by and about authors published in the Virago Modern Classics.

'Good news for everyone writing and reading today' – *Hilary Mantel*

'A continuingly magnificent imprint' – *Joanna Trollope*

'The Virago Modern Classics have reshaped literary history and enriched the reading of us all. No library is complete without them' – *Margaret Drabble*

VIRAGO MODERN CLASSICS
&
CLASSIC NON-FICTION

Some of the authors included in these two series –

Elizabeth von Arnim, Dorothy Baker, Pat Barker, Nina Bawden,
Nicola Beauman, Sybille Bedford, Jane Bowles, Kay Boyle,
Vera Brittain, Leonora Carrington, Angela Carter, Willa Cather,
Colette, Ivy Compton-Burnett, E.M. Delafield, Maureen Duffy,
Elaine Dundy, Nell Dunn, Emily Eden, George Egerton,
George Eliot, Miles Franklin, Mrs Gaskell,
Charlotte Perkins Gilman, George Gissing,
Victoria Glendinning, Radclyffe Hall, Shirley Hazzard,
Dorothy Hewett, Mary Hocking, Alice Hoffman,
Winifred Holtby, Janette Turner Hospital, Zora Neale Hurston,
Elizabeth Jenkins, F. Tennyson Jesse, Molly Keane,
Margaret Laurence, Maura Laverty, Rosamond Lehmann,
Rose Macaulay, Shena Mackay, Olivia Manning, Paule Marshall,
F.M. Mayor, Anaïs Nin, Kate O'Brien, Olivia, Grace Paley,
Mollie Panter-Downes, Dawn Powell, Dorothy Richardson,
E. Arnot Robertson, Jacqueline Rose, Vita Sackville-West,
Elaine Showalter, May Sinclair, Agnes Smedley, Dodie Smith,
Stevie Smith, Nancy Spain, Christina Stead, Carolyn Steedman,
Gertrude Stein, Jan Struther, Han Suyin, Elizabeth Taylor,
Sylvia Townsend Warner, Mary Webb, Eudora Welty,
Mae West, Rebecca West, Edith Wharton, Antonia White,
Christa Wolf, Virginia Woolf, E.H. Young

THE WEATHER IN THE STREETS

Rosamond Lehmann

'No English writer has told of the pains of women in love more truly or more movingly than Rosamond Lehmann' – **Marghanita Laski**

Olivia Curtis, heroine of *Invitation to the Waltz*, is now ten years older. She lives in a tiny house in London eking out a hand-to-mouth existence among writers and artists. With a disastrous marriage behind her, Olivia is still vulnerable and open to love. By chance she meets again the son of the glittering family whose dance she went to all those years ago: Rollo Spencer, handsome, rich, and married. Suddenly, irrevocably, her life is changed to one of secret meetings, brief phone calls and perfect obedience to the rules of clandestine love. She learns, as so many have before her, how harsh life can be for those who love not wisely, but too well.